STILL

LIFE

WITH

PLUMS

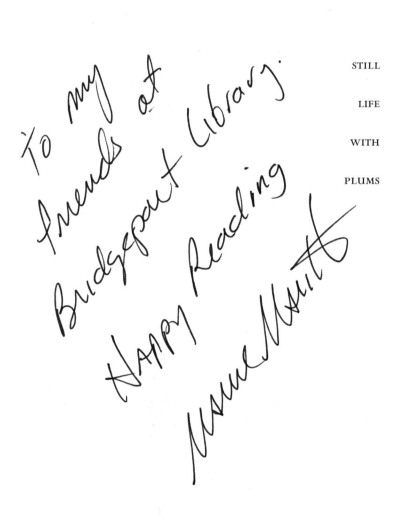

Still life with plums

SHORT STORIES

MARIE MANILLA

Vandalia Press

MORGANTOWN 2010

VANDALIA PRESS, MORGANTOWN 26506

Copyright 2010 by Marie Manilla
First edition published 2010 by Vandalia Press

18 17 16 15 14 13 12 11 10   1 2 3 4 5 6 7 8 9

ISBN-10: 1-933202-60-2 / ISBN-13: 978-1-933202-60-0
(alk. paper)

Library of Congress Cataloguing-in-Publication Information
Manilla, Marie.
Still life with plums : a collection of short stories / by Marie Manilla.
-- 1st ed.
p.   cm.
ISBN-13: 978-1-933202-60-0 (pbk. : alk. paper)
ISBN-10: 1-933202-60-2 (pbk. : alk. paper)
I. Title.
PS3613.A5456S75 2010
813'.6--dc22
Library of Congress Control Number: 2010004710

The following stories first appeared in these publications: "Amnesty." *Prairie Schooner*, 1997; "Childproof." *Calyx, A Journal of Art and Literature by Women*, 2008; "Counting Backwards." *Mississippi Review*, 1996; "Crystal City." *The Chicago Tribune*, 2003; "Distillation." *Carve Magazine*, 2003; "Get Ready." *The Long Story*, 2005; "Grooming." *Writers' Dojo*, 2009; "Hand. Me. Down." *Kestrel*, 2009; "The Wife You Wanted." *Portland Review*, 2009.

Cover Image: "Still Life with Plum," by Reyes Ortega Fernandez.
Courtesy of the artist's estate.

For Elaine Manilla,
who believed in me even before I was born

◆

For Don Primerano, my true north

Acknowledgments

I am deeply grateful to the journals that originally published these stories and to their respective editors who uttered the sweet word: *Yes!* Thank you, too, to all the kind people at West Virginia University Press who saw something good in these pages. I am indebted to the Rogues, phenomenal writers all, who helped me shape my prose and always kept me honest: Laura Bentley, Zoë Ferraris, Paul Martin, John Van Kirk, Mary Sansom, Leslie Birdwell, Shannon Butler, and Charles Lloyd. A thousand blessings to my mother, Elaine Manilla, my biggest fan. There is a special prize in paradise for my husband, Don Primerano, who endures living with this often-unhinged writer with such unflappable grace.

Table of Contents

Hand. Me. Down.

HOLY THURSDAY, 1965, I squatted over the heater vent in the kitchen picking knee scabs when my father's voice boomed from down the hall: "You kids get in the car!" His reverberating diktat roused a pummeling of footsteps up from the dank cement basement where the KKK tortured crickets or mice or my younger brother, Duff. The KKK was an apt acronym for my three older brothers, terrorists all, Kevin, Kieran, and Killian, ages twelve through fourteen. At the top of the stairs, the KKK banged out the back door and skittered and slipped up the muddy hill, their great escape unfoiled since my parents had lost control over them long before. The storm door squealed shut behind them in the April drizzle. Duff started to follow, testing his six-year-old mettle, but Killian roared: "Not you!"

Duff slumped there, eyes welling.

Mom wiped crumbs from the supper table and recentered the doily and bowl of emerald glass balls, the ones I tried to juggle when no one was looking.

Dad thumped down the hall sliding his scary belt through the loops on his waistband. "Where are the girls?" he muttered, though I was crouching right there, one of his girls. I looked too much like him, a Black Irish reminder of his father's mean joke: *Who'd yer mother bed to squeeze out the black-assed loiks-a-yew?* Mostly Grandpa lobbed this insult at my dusky father. The first time he flung it at me, however, when he was out of earshot I whined to my mother: "I'm not black."

"Of course you're not, Doreen." She stopped darning a sock and patted her knee, a rare invitation. Once I was settled on her lap, she spun a fantasy about Spanish sailors in a sixteenth-century Armada who set off to invade England. The Armada shipwrecked off the Irish coast, however, leaving a few water-logged survivors struggling for shore. The Irish women took pity on the pathetic crew and soon they married and started a dark-skinned, dark-eyed bloodline.

"That's rubbish," Grandpa O'Leary snarled from the hall. "She's kin to Irish colonizers who mixed with those West Indie, Montserrat niggers."

Mom sat there, stunned, and it took her four months to convince me that I was as white as my older sisters, nearly, who were not only twins, but willowy, pale-skinned, blue-eyed fairies like Mom.

"Change your shirt," Mom whispered to me as Dad buckled his belt.

I knew better than to grumble in front of Dad, so I scuffed to the room I shared with my ethereal older sisters, my narrow twin bed looking like a lone dinghy beside their luxury liner of a French Provincial queen. Still, it was better than the two sets of bunk beds crammed into the boys' room, the wall beside Duff's mattress slathered with dried boogers because that was the KKK's designated booger wall.

My eleven-year-old sisters sat shoulder to shoulder on the upholstered bench in front of the vanity we inherited from Dad's mother along with the luxury liner queen, combing their golden tresses, the blunt-cut ends skimming their backsides.

"It looks better parted on the left," Mary said to Meg. They lifted identical combs to re-part their hair and secure the corn-silk locks with matching barrettes.

I slid open the closet to dig through the box of clothes I had recently inherited from a neighbor girl three years my senior. Her leftovers would smother my sisters, whose slight shirts and pencil-leg pants would never accommodate me. I found a striped turtleneck, faded from washing, but new to me, and punched my melon head through the taut opening. It only choked a little. Hunching forward, I tried to wedge between the twins and peer into the vanity to see just how unkempt my own wiry mane was, if I needed a brush or my fingers would suffice.

My sisters pressed their shoulders together more tightly, a bony gate slamming. "Use the mirror in the bathroom!" they jointly bleated.

Mom doled out coats and scarves from the hall closet and we crowded there tugging and grunting, buttoning and zipping. Duff and I stole peeks of Dad's face trying to decode the pucker of his mouth, the squint of his eye. Dad wedged his Sunday wingtips into slide-on galoshes which sent Duff, another Black Irish disappointment, rummaging through the mishmash of snow boots and sneakers at the bottom of the closet for his outgrown rain boots. When he found them he backed out and plopped against the closed bathroom door trying to yank them on over his shoes. He groaned with effort, biting his lower lip, and finally succeeded, though he had the right boot on the left foot, the left on the right. He saw his mistake and his face collapsed, but he stood up anyway since Dad was already banging through the front door. "Hurry it up!"

Duff tried to walk, his mouth pulling tight against the pain that was still better than the sting of a whipping.

"Sit down," I whispered, yanking off one boot, then the other, before ramming them correctly in place.

Duff held out his hand and I tugged him upright and outside where Mom and the twins huddled under an umbrella and scuttled down the front steps.

Dad opened the driver's side door, his diagonally striped necktie fluttering up and over his shoulder. Dad never slicked up for the annual trek to collect Mom's mother from the train station, so I knew his attire had to do with our impending car ride. Sliding behind the wheel was still a novelty to him—to all of us—since we had recently acquired our first automobile, a glorious elevation into solid middle class even if the car was used.

It was a black 1955 Ford Country Squire station wagon with faux wood paneling on the doors and tailgate. It sported wide whitewalls and blunted tail fins cradling round taillights. The Squire was top-of-the-line when it rolled out of the factory and into Uncle Merritt's driveway. By the time it rumbled down to us the slick black paint had faded, the decaled wood finish was dimpled with dents, the whitewalls scuffed and gray, and one of the taillights was cracked. Still, we were happy to get it and it could seat nine—our number exactly when our complement was complete—since it was also equipped with a rear-facing bench seat in the cargo area—the designated slot for Duff and me. We were the youngest of the O'Leary brood and thus had no vote, not that any of us had voting privileges besides Dad, not even Mom.

Mom and Dad sat up front, the twins behind them, and Duff and I settled into the rear, kneeling forward on the seat, bums on our heels, so we could avoid motion sickness. Dad started the engine which choked and coughed and finally held steady so that he could back out of the driveway, tailpipe farting blue smoke. Dad steered down our street and I craned to look at Easter decorations taped in our neighbors' plate glass windows: giant cardboard eggs and bunnies and crucifixes. I caught sight of commotion between the Franks' and Hollanders' houses. Three shadowy figures lobbed eggs or rocks or dog turds at the second-floor window of Gary Hollander's room, a hare-lipped, mildly-retarded teen who wore his pants too high and a girl's pink watch. The three goons were my brothers and I was delighted to see them leveling their thuggery at someone other than Duff, or more precisely, me.

The KKK learned early on not to target the twins, Dad's green-house beauties whose slightest pouts and pointed fingers would earn stripes to the KKK's backsides when they were young enough to catch. Duff and I learned that our best defense was invisibility and Duff spent hours twisted inside the tight cabinet beneath the bathroom sink. In warm weather I played in the woods; in winter I climbed through the trapdoor in the hall ceiling to the attic and pretended I was a gymnast tiptoeing back and forth on the nar-row boards, trying not to fall into the insulation that would leave me scratching for days. Or worse, smash my foot through the ceil-ing which would incur harsher penalties. We couldn't hide forever, though, and the KKK's preferred torture for Duff included Indian rub burns and holding him down while they related gruesome details of how they killed various birds, squirrels, turtles, and frogs. True or not, the cruel exploits left Duff's face sticky from snot and tears, and I think if given the choice he would have chosen the rub burn every time. Our family never owned a pet.

Their favored torture for me was bending my fingers backward toward my wrist until I cried Stupid-Ugly, their nickname for me. I tried to endure it, keep my face placid as I recited multiplication tables in my head. *2 x 2 = 4; 4 x 4 = 16.* But I hadn't yet mastered the art of disassociation and eventually I would concede: "Stupid-Ugly. Stupid-Ugly. *Stupid-Ugly!*"

I don't know if Dad spied the KKK between the houses, but he barreled out of our neighborhood, windshield wipers squeaking, leaving behind his immune sons whose hides and dispositions had finally thickened under Dad's repetitive belt- and tongue-lashings.

"Mother will love the car, Dolan," Mom said, pulling a compact from her purse to powder her dishwater-steamed face. She peered into the mirrored disk in the evening's last light and tried to fluff her hair and apply lipstick because she never had one single minute to gussy up at home.

Dad grunted, spine straightening as if he'd forgotten about the dents and dings and his older brother's smug mug when he handed over the keys. "Don't ride the clutch," Uncle Merritt had said. "Change the oil more than once a year. And don't ever let those wild boys drive it!"

"Maybe she'll buy us new Easter dresses!" Mary said, a thought that set the twins shivering, and me, too, but for different reasons. I remembered too well the previous year's shopping disaster, all that purple chiffon and itchy lace because the three girls had to match— though I was no match for my sisters.

"Don't you girls pester Grandma," Mother said, craning around to better glare at the twins, her eyes more fearful than challenging. Clearly she remembered my father's ear-steaming rant when he discovered that his mother-in-law had clothed his daughters in a grander style than he could ever afford.

"Didn't your mother just make you new dresses?" Dad said, his black eyes peering into the rearview, a look that would have me stuttering but that had no effect on the twins.

"Nobody wears homemade clothes anymore," Meg said.

I looked at the back of Mom's head, her shoulders stooped as if she were still hunkered over the sewing machine with the bobbin that routinely clotted with thread. The way her eyebrows furrowed whenever she tried to untangle the knotted mess, as if she wanted to hoist the blasted machine over her head and hurl it through the side window.

"Your mother wears handmade dresses," Dad said. "What's good enough for her should be good enough for the loiks-a-yew."

"Then let *her* wear them," the twins spat.

The turtleneck pinched my neck as Duff and I glanced at each other, both of us holding our breath. I don't think Mom was breathing either.

"Spoiled brats," Dad finally muttered, his voice firm, but the crinkle around his eyes betrayed pride in his mouthy offspring.

I marveled once more at the twins' nerve.

"Your father called today," Mom said, tugging her earlobe in that frantic way she always did when she delivered bad news.

Dad's shoulders drew up. "What for?"

"He wants you to pick him up after Easter mass and bring him to our house for dinner."

Dad hunkered over the steering wheel, jaw grating back and forth. "Something wrong with his car?"

"He didn't say."

"He can't drive two miles?" Dad said, voice raspy.

Mother didn't answer because what could she say?

"Why can't he eat over at Merritt's?"

Even I knew the answer to that. The last time the extended family gathered at Uncle Merritt's for a meal, Grandpa knocked over his water glass. He mechanically drew his hand back and swiped at his wife who would have been sitting beside him if she hadn't bluntly died a month before. Instead, Grandpa struck Merritt's eight-year-old daughter who wailed like the banshee she was.

Aunt Sally swung around from the stove, spatula in hand. "Did he hit you?" she asked her sniveling daughter. "Did you hit her?" she spat at Grandpa.

Mom and Dad slunk down in their seats as Uncle Merritt thundered up his basement steps, bottles of homemade beer clinking in his arms.

"Your father hit her!" Aunt Sally squealed.

Uncle Merritt gawped at the red handprint blooming across his daughter's cheek.

"Do something!" Aunt Sally implored.

Uncle Merritt looked at his father, his brother, his wife, his poor little slobbering daughter, the pathetic sight of her turning his neck splotchy, but that only made me want to kick her under the table and yell: *Don't show it!*

Uncle Merritt peered down at his father and seethed: "I don't care if you did just lose Ma. No one hits my daughter. No one! I want you out of my house!"

Grandpa's eyes rounded as if he couldn't believe the sudden expulsion, and neither could I. We'd just gotten our salads. Grandpa slammed his fist on the table, water glasses trembling, pushed out of his chair, and stomped to the front door, but not before thumping my dad's ear and growling: "Dolan! Get in the car!"

Dad shot up. Grandpa was our ride, after all. "Come on, Marge," he said to my mother who was shoveling in peaches and cottage cheese as fast as she could.

"Not you," Aunt Sally said to Mom. "I'll give you and the kids a ride home after supper. Stay, please."

"Marge!" Dad seethed. "Get the kids in the car!"

Mom cringed and we all tugged the napkins from our collars and piled them on our empty plates.

At the curb, Grandpa raised his fist to the house. "I'll not stay where I'm not wanted!" he railed before smacking Dad once more. Dad's face paled and he whipped around to yank Kieran by the elbow and hurl him into the backseat of Grandpa's sedan, followed by Killian, then Kevin, their bony shoulders and skulls clacking together like coconuts. The twins quietly slid onto Mom and Dad's laps in the front seat, and Duff and I balanced on the KKK's knobby knees for the grueling ride home. That was the night the KKK devised the rubber band/emery board/coat hanger torture.

Eighteen months after that, in our new old car on the way to the train station, Dad stopped at a traffic light. I looked out the window as two wet dogs rooted for scraps from a tipped-over, rusted-out trash can. They fought over a wad of tinfoil, the smaller one winning, and I was glad.

Meg fidgeted in her seat and finally whined, "Why can't we take the train to visit Grandma? She invites us every summer."

Every time Grandma visited she prodded my father: *Dolan, let Marge and the girls come to Pittsburgh. Surely you and the boys can fend for yourselves for two weeks.*

Even I was afraid of that notion, imagining a mass grave in the backyard upon our return. Filled with exactly whose bones I wouldn't hazard to guess, but maybe then I could have my own room.

"Grandma doesn't want you squawking brats up there," Dad said.

"She does, too," Mary wailed. "She wants us to move in forever!"

Grandma never told me that, or Dad, I'm sure. The light turned green and Dad emitted a low growl before pressing the gas as he no doubt considered the tense week we were about to endure. The trouble Grandma Lorraine always stirred. The only perk for me was that I would be relegated to the living room sofa where I could pretend to sleep while Mom and Grandma sipped highballs in the kitchen after Dad went to bed. Invariably Grandma would slur: *Why did you have to marry a coal miner, for God's sake,* a puzzling dig at our West Virginia roots since Dad was a telephone lineman and Grandma knew that.

Truthfully, I had never seen a coal mine or a miner in all my nine years except on TV. Often a newsman would stand before a mineshaft as helmeted men hopped onto a contraption that would drive them into the gaping black hole. I knew those men and their families lived in a strip of dingy company houses on the east end of town. Shantytown, everyone called it. I had also seen coal trains winding through our shadow-filled valley, whistles howling, car after car piled high with the glistening black stuff that would bounce out and ping like popcorn against the iron rails. The miners' kids went to my school and on my very first day of first grade Meg and Mary impressed upon me that I should never talk to a coal kid, not even to borrow a pencil or a piece of paper. If at all possible I shouldn't breathe the air around them because their skin was cootified with noxious mine fumes which would turn my skin even darker than it already was.

I didn't talk to the coal kids, but I watched them run in packs on the playground, their lungs laboring, their skin ruddy. I stole peeks of them greedily eating together in the cafeteria, never leaving one crumb. Afterwards, a few of them hovered around as the hair-netted lunch lady scraped off uneaten morsels from other kids' trays. When her back was turned they reached their hands into the bin of mangled food to steal hunks of cheese, half-eaten sandwiches. Coal niggers, the KKK called them, both black and white, after routinely chasing them away from the school bus stop. *Run on home you little snot-nosed, soot-skinned, coal niggers!* More than once they added: *You too, Doreen!*

The twins started rocking in their seat, chirping about Grandma's visit, hoping she would paint their nails and let them wear her jewelry and for the millionth time describe her two-story house which had four bedrooms, two full bathrooms, and a solarium: a glassed-in porch filled with African violets, white wicker furniture, and streaming beams of sunlight. If we ever did make it to Pittsburgh I would muscle my way to the solarium and stake my claim. The twins could have all four bedrooms for all I cared.

"Maybe she's bringing the piano!" Mary said, a reference to the upright Baldwin Grandma offered to ship down so the twins could take lessons.

"Like we have a place to put it," Meg sniped.

Dad grumbled at this gibe at the cramped quarters he provided. He clicked on the left turn signal and paused for oncoming traffic at the entrance to the train station parking lot. The windshield wipers squeaked. The turn signal tick-ticked.

"I hope those boys aren't into my cheese ball," Mom mumbled to herself, a valid concern since the KKK devoured everything, regardless.

"They'd better not be," Dad said, probably wondering, like me, if they were balancing buckets of mice on doorjambs or hiding copperheads under Grandma's blankets.

The twins pressed their fingers to their chins and in their best Grandma imitation said: "What those boys need is a good military school. They're out of control, Marge! Completely out of control!"

Dad looked in the rearview at his treasured girls, though it didn't look as if he treasured them that second.

Meg leaned over the front seat—a brave maneuver, I thought. "Mom, Mrs. Ottman puts pineapple rings and cherries on her ham—"

"And pokes cloves into it," Mary added, leaning forward, too. "Can we do that this year?"

Mom started tugging her earlobe. "That sounds pretty, but—"

"Those damn boys better not be fooling with my Easter ham," Dad spat.

"And brown sugar!" Meg said. "She rolls the whole thing in brown sugar mixed with Coca-Cola!"

"That sounds fun," Mom said, pulling her fleshy earlobe nearly down to her shoulder. "But I thought we would eat something different this year."

"Something different!" we all said, even Dad. Even Duff.

My little brother looked forward to Easter ham even more than the chocolate bunnies and Marshmallow Peeps the KKK would inevitably *trade* for their black jellybeans. Of course no one anticipated it more than Dad. He made an elaborate production of sharpening his knife and pulling down the wire ham stand from its place on the highest shelf in the kitchen as if he were a priest pulling the Eucharist from the tabernacle during mass. It might have been the singular joy Duff and Dad shared. Emboldened by hunger, Duff would hover around as Dad positioned the ham firmly in its stand before sawing off slice after slice and piling them onto the good china platter. Every now and then Dad would slide a piece into his mouth and offer one to Duff. "Atta boy," Dad would say. "That'll put muscles on you."

I could hear Mom exhaling even from where I sat. "Actually, we're going to have roast chicken this year—stuffed with wild rice! Doesn't that sound exotic?"

"Wild rice?" said Meg and Mary, plopping back in their seats, practically cracking me in the nose, and Duff, since were still leaning over their seatback.

"Wild rice!" said Dad.

"Everyone has ham for Easter," Mom said, flapping a dismissive hand, pushing out a laugh that sounded more like a sob.

"We can't have chicken for Easter dinner," Dad said to himself.

"We can't have chicken for Easter dinner!" he said to the rest of us. "My *father* is coming, for Christ's sake. And your mother!"

"They both like chi—"

"You know what Merritt is serving?" Dad railed.

By the way Mom's shoulders jerked I knew she was bunching up the hem of her skirt as she often did.

"Do you know what Merritt is serving?" Dad asked her again.

"No," Mom said.

"A standing rib roast *and* ham. *And* ham!"

"What's a standing rib roast?" Mary asked.

"Why aren't we having ham, Marge?" Dad said. "Tell me. What made you think we shouldn't have a ham?"

Mom sat there, pleating her hem, looking at her lap.

"Marge! Why aren't we having a ham!"

"Because the boys needed new shoes," she whispered.

All the air was sucked out of the car, all sound, too, until Meg opened her fat mouth and said: "We can't afford anything nice."

Dad jerked around in his seat, hand raised as if he were going to strike one of his precious lilies, but a car horn wailed from behind. Detoured by our ham plight, my father had missed numerous opportunities to turn into the parking lot.

Dad shook his fist at the driver behind us. "Shut up!" he yelled. "I'll stay here all night if I want to!"

I turned to look out the back window as the burly driver honked again, a long, lingering wail followed by a staccato burst from yet another car stacked up behind him.

Even with the windows closed I heard the burly man howl: "Make the goddamn turn!"

Dad started to open his door but Mom grabbed his arm. "Dolan, Mom's train is due any minute."

Duff and I bent over to scan the station. We always looked forward to waiting on the platform, leaning as far over the painted yellow line as we could before some black porter tugged us back by the elbows. *You kids don't cross the line, now. Don't want to get hit by the train.* We wanted to be the first to spot the train's white headlight in the distance barreling toward us, followed by the squeal of the brakes as the train neared, growing larger and larger, a slick, coal-burning, black monster that awed us completely.

The man behind us leaned on his horn once more. "Move that hunk-a-junk before I rear-end your ass out of the way!"

Dad hunched down in his seat and punched the gas pedal, hard, sending Duff and me into the cargo hold, but instead of turning into the parking lot, Dad drove straight.

Duff and I righted ourselves as Dad veered right onto Main Street and headed east, revving the engine as if he were torquing his nerve.

"Where are we going?" Duff whispered to me.

I shrugged, turtleneck tightening as we sped away from the station, from Grandma's train maybe pulling in that very minute, her face pressed against the window of the passenger car as she looked for her daughter and her daughter's brood.

"Dolan, where are we going?" Mom asked, hands gripping the dashboard.

"Can't afford an Easter ham," Dad seethed.

The windshield wipers whined and the ignored turn signal tick-ticked.

"Mother's train," Mom said, the words thin and wispy.

"Can't fit a piano in our house," Dad said. "I'll show you kids what real poor looks like."

Meg and Mary looked at each other practically nose to nose. I wondered if they were as alarmed as Duff and me until Mary mouthed: *I'll show you what real poor looks like!* which sent Meg into a giggling fit.

"You kids be quiet back there!" Dad said, propelling us forward like a torpedo barreling over winding roads that dipped and swelled, my stomach dipping and swelling, too. My mind mechanically calculated numbers to distract my quivering gut. *5 x 5 = 25; 6 x 6 = 36.*

Dad finally slowed down and I knew where we were by the row of narrow boxes pretending to be houses. Shantytown.

There they were. The stuff of myths. A dozen of the tiniest houses I had ever seen all lined up in a row. Each box was maybe twelve feet wide by thirty feet long. Even our house was bigger. I tried to imagine the internal layout, if there were walls that separated one room from the next, or if everything was out in the open: unmade beds, the kitchen table, the commode.

Dad stopped the car in the middle of the road and rolled down his window to better gape at the spectacle, the wet wind blowing in and whirling around the car, ruffling his hair, and Mom's. The twins huddled together in the middle seat, their blonde hair whipping Duff and me in the face, stinging our eyes. They tried to capture the loose tendrils and hold them in place.

"Close the window!" they yelled.

"Take a good look," Dad said. "Maybe then you'll be grateful for what you have."

Meg and Mary didn't take a good look, but I sure did. There were lights on in windows and I saw people inside going about their lives, oblivious to the carload of gawkers appraising their poverty. In one house five kids were crammed onto a couch, flickering lights from the black and white TV pulsing against their skin. In another a whole family was squeezed around the supper table, elbows and mouths flapping wildly until they all started laughing, every single one of them, even a fat-cheeked toddler strapped into a high chair.

"How would you brats like to live out here?" Dad said, jutting his chin at the display.

Duff gripped my knee. "Us too?" he whispered, tears already rimming his frantic eyes as he peered into the dilapidated shacks, no doubt searching for a tight cabinet under a bathroom sink.

"You kids have it pretty good," Dad said. "A nice house. A new car."

"I'm not moving in with a bunch of coal niggers," Meg muttered.

Mom whipped around in her seat. "What did you say?"

Meg didn't have time to answer because Mary pointed her finger at a lanky boy trotting up the mud path that served as a sidewalk. "That's Mark Bailey!"

"I didn't know he lived down here," Meg said about their classmate. "His daddy's not a miner."

"His father works with you, doesn't he Dolan?" Mom said, trying to deflate the tension.

Dad looked at the kid ambling up the front steps of one of those houses and entering without knocking. Dad gripped the steering wheel and nestled his rump in the seat. "That's not Bailey's house."

"Sure it is," Mom said. "That's Hank sitting right there in the living room."

"In his underwear!" Meg said, exploding in laughter.

"He probably can't afford pajamas," Mary said.

Dad slunk even lower. "You kids think this is funny? I'll leave you here right now," he said, a hint of fierceness drained from his voice.

"I see London. I see France," Meg said, snorting.

"You hear me?" Dad said to the twins who only tipped their heads together and giggled, their hair wildly whipping. "I'll leave you here right now!" Dad said.

"Nuh uh," Meg said. "We'll move to Pittsburgh and live in Grandma's solarium!"

"No!" I blurted, immediately clamping my hand over my mouth.

"The hell you will," Dad said, fierceness fully inflated once more. "I'll toss you to the curb this very minute! I mean it!"

"I mean it!" the twins echoed as if they didn't believe a word he said. "We'll sleep on her wicker couches and sip lemonade in the sun!" Mary said.

Dad twisted around in his seat to better glare at his prized girls, his power circling the drain. The twins lifted their impervious noses and the only thing left for Dad to do was look past them at Duff and me trembling there, believing him utterly.

"You hear me back there, Duff! Doreen! If you two don't appreciate what I provide I'll put you out right here and let you fend for yourselves! You hear me?"

7 x 7 = 49.

"Yes," I answered for both of us since Duff had no voice to offer.

"I'll do it, too!" Dad swiveled back around and looked at Mom who was slouching so far forward she looked headless.

I spun around in the rear-facing bench seat, the turtleneck a tight hand wrapped around my throat as I glared out the back window. Dad sped away, the row of shanty houses disappearing in the gray rain as if we were tunneling deeper and deeper into a mineshaft, away from Grandma's bright solarium filled with streaming beams of sunlight that my sisters had already claimed.

Duff turned around, too, still trembling, and nestled close to my side. Too close.

"He doesn't mean it, does he?" Duff whispered to me.

I looked over at my little brother trying to twine his fingers through mine. But looking at him only made my gut clench until I felt something crack open deep inside. A burning wave rushed through my stomach, legs, arms, head, a hot heat that demanded release, the pressure building as the turn signal ticked, the windshield wipers screamed, the turtleneck tried to choke me to death.

The only thing I could do was wrap my fingers around Duff's closed fist and start squeezing. He looked up at me, startled at first, accepting, even as I squeezed harder and harder.

"Stop it," he whispered, finally trying to tug free.

But I wouldn't let go. I leaned close to his face and the more he whimpered the better I felt, so I squeezed even harder, *8 x 8 = 64; 9 x 9 = 81,* imagining his delicate finger bones splintering. I was immune to his pleas: "Stop it, Doreen. It hurts."

Which only made me angrier so I leaned close to his ear and seethed: "You're nothing but a stupid-ugly Montserrat nigger. You know that?" *10 x 10 = 100; 11 x 11 = 121.* "A stupid-ugly Montserrat nigger. Say it. Say it. *Say it!*"

Childproof

This bridal shower sucks, truly, and my shorts are too tight—my *fat* shorts, pinching my belly rolls (yes, plural), my crotch, and I can hear my ex-husband shouting across three states: *I can't believe you went out in public wearing that!* He is right again, naturally, since I am once again underdressed in a roomful of shift dresses and well-ironed skorts. Tidy hairdos and pert sandals. No three-second ponytails or clodhopper Birkenstocks—other than mine, of course. So I hunker over a bowl of mixed nuts, elbows on the table, picking out cashews, every single one, never mind my assigned game partner Aaaandreaaaa's (that's how she pronounced it, I swear) disgruntled snorts as I ram spit-coated fingers into the legumes to rummage and root. *Get your own damn nuts.*

"My door prize," I say, indicating the bowl, hard-won cashew glob stuck in my teeth, I'm sure, but I don't care as I ogle Aaaandreaaaa's bow-tied photo album *and* a potted geranium, her legitimate trophies for knowing not only how the impending bride and groom met (at a Red's game), but their honeymoon destination as well (Curaçao).

I suck the salt from my fingertips in a most unladylike fashion, annoying Andi—my new de-snootified pet name for Aaaandreaaaa—further, though she's already quite peeved at me for not playing nice during the introduction game. I lied every single time.

Andi dealt the first index card inked with the hand-scrawled query: How do you know the bride?

I'm her bridal consultant. She flew me in all the way from gay Paree.

No! Andi said, eyeing my only slightly wrinkled, dog-hair-coated T-shirt.

Oui! At the reception we'll be serving snail brains in a light cream sauce.

Her patience waned as the interrogation persisted. Are you married?

But of course. Le nom de mon mari est Jacques Cousteau.

Do you have any children?

No. I can't stand clingy people. Thus ending the tête-à-tête.

Maid-of-Honor announces that there will be yet another game.

Oh, joy.

"Oh, goodie," says Andi.

M-O-H has to yell over the cackling horde of thirty woman gathered in this dank church basement, cerulean and fuchsia crepe paper looped from the drop ceiling, smashed strawberries and bakery-cake frosting smeared across the linoleum. "What will the happy couple name their first baby?"

I poise to guffaw, but someone beats me to it. "They're not even married yet! And maybe they don't want children!"

It's a woman standing slightly apart from the madding crowd, in shorts and huaraches, not Birkenstocks, exactly, but close enough for me, and it's empowering to know that I'm not the only smart-ass in the room. She's brave to bellow that out loud in front of these optimistic women, some with toddlers or infants strapped to various body parts. "Hear, hear!" I add. We tip our punch cups at each other and take sailor swigs while several of the *ladies* roll their eyes.

Someone yodels, "Is it a girl or a boy?"

"One of each!" M-O-H jubilantly predicts.

"I know this! I know this!" Andi trills, cupping a hand over her paper so she can scribe the names in secret.

This pisses me off, of course, so I pull my paper close to my chest and drape an entire meaty forearm across it as a fortress. Let's see. Appropriate names for the happy couple's twins: Bonnie and Clyde, Julius and Ethel Rosenberg, Harold and Maude. The last movie pair not *real*, exactly, but then neither are the twins, not yet anyway, maybe not ever.

I look at the twin-less bride-to-be, Pam, the dog groomer I hired seven months ago to work in my kennel, one of three groomers now since business is growing. Opening my own canine *salon* was my only defense against being perpetually scheduled to work nights, holidays, and weekends in every other job I've endured on the planet, because childless women apparently have nothing else to fill their dull, meaningless lives. If I'm going to have to pull long hours, which I do, at least the profits are mine. And now there sits blushing Pam, the reason I got sucked into this festive torture—employee morale, yadda-yadda. That and the promise that it wasn't a fancy affair, chicken salad and carrot sticks. The sweet lure of cake. Pam got the food right, but the attire, well . . . . I again try to tug down my shorts, drawing Andi's attention to my thighs, two jumbo rolls of rippled white tripe, then we both look at her well-toned, tanning-bed thighs, the comparison test, half the size of mine. She wins again. *Bitch.*

While Andi is distracted by her winning gams, a woman across the room belts out the twins' correct names (Madison for a girl, Aidan for a boy—or vice versa) capturing the grand prize: a gi-gundo shrink-wrapped basket of toiletries (which I recognize from Sam's Club, thank you very much—though I only went there once, with my mother, under duress).

Andi is sorely disappointed and her loss makes me feel all light and fluttery.

I stand to announce, "I'm going to the ladies," waistband of my shorts cutting furiously into my punch-bloated bladder.

"Fine," says Andi. As I turn to leave I think I hear her mutter, "Thank God."

I am directed to the bathroom by several women in the kitchen with their arms up to the elbows in dishwater, keeping up with the punch glasses. Church ladies, I can tell, because I am a churchgoer (yes, women without children often believe in a Supreme Being). I have been mightily snubbed by church women. Passed over as Sunday school teacher and Vacation Bible School director because what could I possibly know about children? Point taken, though I've certainly bought enough Girl Scout cookies and Boy Scout popcorn from those same church children to support the troops. I also take offense at only being assigned prepackaged food for potlucks: potato chips, maybe, or a bag of ice. Childless women certainly don't cook. *Oy.*

When I come back through, waistband no longer feeling so snug (leaving the distinct possibility for more cake), one of those hallowed women is struggling to pull a trash bag from the can, her spindly, bone-density-loss arms no match for the Hefty overstuffed with paper plates, foam cups, plastic two-liters, and empty Kroger containers for coleslaw and potato salad (even I could have managed that deli-served fare). "Don't believe in recycling?" I mutter.

"What's that, dear?" she asks.

I don't have the heart to repeat it because the woman looks spent. "Allow me," I say.

"Thank you, precious," she says. "Now don't hurt yourself."

I've hoisted 150-pound Mastiffs onto slick metal tables. I lift the trash bag out effortlessly and even tie off the top. "Where to?" I ask, because I can't imagine this worn soul lugging it very far.

"Right outside that door," she says, patting my arm. "You're a treasure."

Precious! Treasure! Wow. I float on those epithets all the way outside into the heat where metal cans are lined up in the side yard. I plunk the bag in, settle the lid, and turn toward the ring of children sitting in a circle in the grass. They're blowing bubbles and making clover chains, and I recognize some of them from inside. Two teenage girls have been roped into babysitting. I hope they're getting paid, at least, and aren't just collecting God points, jewels for their crowns, as my late grandma would say.

I remember when all my school friends started babysitting, earning money for the movies or a sundae at Nierman's. I especially remember the day Mrs. Goebel called to ask if I could watch her two-year-old son. I had to ask Mother first, but her response put the skids on that venture. "Don't be ridiculous," she said. "But tell her you might consider cutting grass." I understood then that I could not be trusted with children. I could, however, preside over turf.

A tremulous voice bleats from the parking lot, "Well crap!" It's one of those church women standing beside a sun-faded Buick, hands on her hips as she surveys the flat left rear tire. She stoops to assess the damage and warbles, "What on earth am I going to do now!"

I scuff through the yard toward her. "Flat tire?" I say, *duh.*

She swivels toward me, no doubt expecting the cavalry, and says, "I've got a tire iron and spare if you know how to use them?"

"Sorry," I say. The closest I've come to automotive repair is adding AAA to my speed dial.

Her disappointment is visible, but she straightens up and sighs, "I have twenty-four-hour road service, though it may take twenty-four hours for them to get here."

We head back into the kitchen, which is abuzz with kitchen activity, and, feeling as though I have let the world down, I belt out, "Anyone know how to change a flat tire?"

"I do." It's my huarache-wearing, loud-mouth comrade pouring an envelope of Kool-Aid into a pitcher. She wipes grape-stained hands down her shorts and says, "Where to?"

The deflated Buick woman re-inflates. "Right out here."

I tag along to offer moral support and watch my mechanically inclined sister hoist the tire iron and jack from the trunk, pry off the hubcap, and start twisting off lug nuts, sinewy muscles straining. Twice I open my mouth to offer assistance, but really, what would be the point. Instead I head back inside and commandeer her Kool-Aid chore, stirring up a whirlpool in the purple liquid with my spoon. I carry the pitcher to the drink table in the fellowship hall just as M-O-H settles Pam on a chair in the middle of the festivities to open her gifts. The sugar-hyped flower girl spins pirouettes beside her, lacy dress billowing out like a bell.

Lucky for me the food table is unattended and now's my chance to grab more cake, ignoring my ex's jibe, *Like you need more cake.* Or is that Mother's voice? *Up yours,* I snarl at both, heading right for the confection, opting for a corner piece with a massive pink flower. I lean against the counter and shovel it in, enjoying the tacky feel of lard frosting coating the roof of my mouth.

Afterwards, I resist the urge for a third piece and fix a to-go plate for Jeremy, my current husband, endowed with a kind, kind heart. The only human who loves me as unconditionally as my four dogs and three cats, a man who lavishes me with praise that I someday hope to believe. I am still very much recovering from Husband Number One, and maybe from Mother, too. Who, by the way, is still angry at me for depriving her of her own mother-of-the-bride moment because her only daughter, her only *child* for that matter, eloped not once, but twice. A scab she picked at as recently as yesterday when she helped me select a shower gift for Pam. Of course I wanted to go to Spencer's for something slightly pornographic, but Mother bribed me into Macy's china department with the promise of a free lunch that would involve red meat *and*, if I truly behaved, beer.

I obliged, a regular angel, even kept my elbows in and my smart-aleck remarks to myself as I scooted past $150 Lenox salt and pepper shakers and napkin rings. I owed Mother that much, or so she always claimed, because I was such a gross disappointment. Of course she never used those words, but she often tells the story of when the doctor first held up my slippery seven pound, eight ounce body (the only minute of my life I was not overweight) and pronounced my gender—*It's a girl!* Mother claimed that my whole life flashed before her eyes.

Not *my* life, it turns out, but my life as her daughter. Days filled with matching dresses, shopping sprees, joint hair appointments, and tea lunches with cucumber sandwiches and delicate cookies that I would primly nibble.

I am not a nibbler—as evidenced by the cashew and cake-snarfing incidents. I hate dresses and pantyhose, white gloves, and clutch purses. I cut my own hair—mostly symmetrically—and, as a child, I liked to splash around in mud puddles when I wasn't playing with fire or sawing off my Barbie dolls' hands. (I preferred Troll dolls, I confess, their stout bow-legged bodies and wild vertical hair a closer fit to the reality that was me.)

Squealing laughter pulls me away from my beloved Trolls to the spectacle before me—poor, poor Pam wearing a paper-plate hat piled high with her shower gifts' bows. She looks at me and shrugs, resigned to the humiliation that comes with the bridal territory. I nod in a manner that suggests I *will* be circulating hyperbolic stories about this around the doggy dryers come Monday morning.

Someone taunts, "She broke another ribbon. She's up to *five* kids now!"

Please don't make us name them, though I can always use the spare names Mother accumulated for the other children she never had (my father, lucky bastard, making his great escape when I was three, even if his freedom only came in the guise of a massive coronary, snuffing out my tadpole siblings too)—Marcia, Helen, Barbara, Stephen, Matthew, and Nicholas. Mother kindly offered—if that's the right word—to let Husband Number One and me have those anointed titles when we started our own family. It's a good thing we lived three states away when she delivered that list over the phone, because we weren't even expecting, or expecting to expect any time soon. Number One had strong feelings about children. Or against them, I should say. Jeremy is softer on the issue. *Whatever you want*, he has said numerous times. *I just want you to be happy*, he says, and I think I believe him.

Someone has taken my seat next to Andi (or perhaps Andi had enough of my shenanigans and bribed them: Pa-lease sit here, won't you? No, she's *not* coming back—and don't touch those nuts!). So I head for three vacant seats at the end of a different table, place settings untainted so I know they're empty, and if I'm lucky, will remain so for the duration. I can be quite anti-social on occasion, surprise-surprise. This is a better seat, actually, closer to the bridal action, where I can inventory the opened gifts and see if there is anything worth borrowing, like that fancy-schmancy espresso machine, or that margarita maker complete with jumbo glasses and a special dish to salt the rims. Now *that's* a gift worth getting. Maybe I should have opted for the shower after all.

But no, I take that back as I assess Pam's other spoils: place settings and flatware and irons and cookbooks. The detritus of a marriage that may not last, and though I'm hopeful for Jeremy and me—I give us a good sixty/forty chance—it's hard to make a quick exit with all that junk piled on one's back. Of course one could always leave it behind, like I did with my first marriage: Grandma's mahogany dresser, that hand-blown cameo vase my best friend sent all the way from West Virginia, my jewelry box, dammit, with Aunt Frankie's brooch and my favorite ankle bracelet. Leaving me to forever wonder if some other woman is wearing that brooch, if she's sliding her underwear and socks into Grandma's dresser, plunking dried roses in my cameo vase.

God help you, I offer to the conjured woman, understanding the bruising price tag that comes with those treasures.

A finger taps my shoulder. "Is anyone sitting here?" It's my huarache-shod, tire-changing hero, and I gratefully blurt, "No! Have a seat!" She pulls in with her fresh plate piled with ample servings, I note, though she is not ample herself by my standards, the weighty infraction reduced when I see the tire smudges on her shorts, the grit under her nails.

"What did I miss?" she asks, mouthful of chicken salad, poor table etiquette endearing her to me even more.

"Most of the cooing-over-the-pricey-gifts," I say.

"Thank God." She nods toward the stack. "Has she opened my case of shoe liners yet?"

"No, but my twelve-pack of air fresheners was a tremendous hit."

"I'm Peggy," she says, not even bothering to wipe off the streak of mayonnaise on her palm before offering her hand.

"Jackie," I say, a blunt version of Jacquelyn, my honest-to-god name. Not Clodda, the fib I offered to Aaaandreaaaa, though a better fit than Jacquelyn, which is far too snobby, my mother's precise intention that, like so many of her expectations, fell flat.

Peggy, I learn, is the groom's sister who owns a bakery in San Diego. *Does it get any better?* I again eye her stomach, only slightly convex, certainly not to the extent mine would be if I were surrounded by cake batter and cookie dough all day—my version of heaven.

I ask her to please, please tell me what a typical workday for her is like, and not to gloss over details like setting the oven temperature or greasing pans. She obliges, spinning a fantasy about baker's chocolate and egg yolks and heavy cream. Caramel glazes and toasted almonds and liqueur-soaked lady fingers. She is a goddess and everyone in the room should bow down to her magnificence.

And then the flower girl pukes—too many pirouettes—replacing the warm, gooey fragrances concocted in my head with the putrid stink of bowel-slung punch and partially digested chicken salad.

Half a dozen women rush to her aid, including Peggy, who lunges off with two words, "Oh, fuck." Another six scatter for wet paper towels, quickly returning to wipe down the girl's face, dress, fingers, and the chunky mess on the floor. Peggy comes back with the now-bawling child in tow.

"It's okay," Peggy says, sitting, hoisting the child onto her lap.

I'm stunned. "Is this . . . is she . . . ?"

"My daughter Emily."

"Oh," is all I can manage, my goddess roped back to earth and now saddled with children.

"My dress!" Emily whines, running her little fingers across the lime stains on her lacy togs.

"That's what Spray 'n Wash is for," Peggy consoles. She leans close to me. "I swear, the child can barely tie her shoes and already she's into high fashion. Didn't get that from *me*," Peggy says, and by the look of her, I believe it, though I can only imagine Mother's dismay if that were me throwing up, not just on my good dress, but in front of the guests: Oh, the humiliation—for her.

Peggy simultaneously rocks Emily into a torpor, eats her potato salad (not put off by the vomit smell still emanating from her child), and delivers a description of a seven-layer chocolate torte, her specialty, with a gooey center that explodes in your mouth when you bite into it. She wants to know about my job too, and though I can't offer up anything as exquisite as volcanic cake, I volunteer my best dog stories, including—Mother still doesn't believe this—my great joy in detailing them with ribbons and tuxedo vests and plastic tiaras.

We yak for an hour, I swear, Peggy painting visions of driving cross-country to attend this shower. Two thousand miles in a car with no relief drivers, on Route 66 no less, all the way to St. Louis, with a side trip to the Grand Canyon and every funky hot dog stand along the way. The woman is describing my top-down, hair-whipping, dream vacation (sans child's car seat) if I only had the guts.

Emily snores, and I am once against stunned to find myself having a real adult conversation with a woman who has a sleeping child draped across her lap, not one who is tugging on Mommy's thigh or smearing oatmeal-coated fingers down her blouse or screaming for a drink, or a cookie, or that seductively placed toy on the lowest shelf in the impulse-buying zone at the grocery store. I don't even flinch when Emily's hand flops over and rests on my forearm, tiny fingers wiggling, and I wonder what she's up to in her sleep: making Easy-Bake cookies, playing chopsticks on the piano.

Emily is not the only surprise. Up comes a boy, maybe seven or eight, with three cherry popsicles clutched in his hands. "Mom!" he says, drawing Peggy's attention to the booty. I love him already because, unlike his spindly sister, he's a chubby kid, looking like Pugsley Addams in his well-worn striped shirt and uneven buzz cut. I watch Peggy's face to see if it collapses the way Mother's did whenever I plodded up to her.

But Peggy just extends an arm toward him. "There's my Toby," she says, drawing him into this maternal tableau. "This is Miss Jackie," she says.

Toby looks at the popsicles in his hands and his face puckers up as he labors over long division. "I only brought three," he says, looking from Emily to Peggy, the other apparent recipients.

"I don't think Emily is up for one right now anyway," Peggy says.

Emily blows a spit bubble in her sleep.

"Okay," Toby whispers, handing mine over first.

"Thank you, sir," I say.

"You're a good man," Peggy says.

Toby delivers some circuitous, non sequitur tale about his exploits in the choir loft, about discovering a box of Jesus puppets, about the wooden-slatted organ pedals. Peggy listens intently, as if he's divulging directions for Blackbeard's treasure, offering encouraging blurbs: *Is that right? Really! How totally cool.*

I marvel at her patient, uncritical attention.

Finally Toby gallops off and Peggy asks quite unexpectedly, "Do you have kids?"

For once I am not irritated by the inquiry. It's an earnest one.

"No," I say, wondering how I should finish, because I always feel compelled to offer an excuse for my childless state. A defense. I have a whole catalogue of answers depending, some absolute lies: That I married too late. That my ovaries are shriveled. That I really don't like babies. Have such a weak stomach that just the thought of poopy diapers and snotty noses sends me gagging, and I don't believe it when all those mothers say: *It's different when it's your own!*

Some truths that I only recently unearthed for Jeremy: That I'm a workaholic, too invested in my kennel and it wouldn't be fair (though Jeremy said he'd be perfectly content as Mr. Mom).

That sometimes fathers escape, and mothers too, even when they stick around.

And there are darker truths—or lies that I have bought into but good—that I barely have the courage to admit to myself, let alone to another human being.

Peggy's eyebrows crinkle and her head cocks to the side, because I'm sure I look as if I am about to deliver a weighty admission, some non-smartass reality coaxed out by the sweet safety of this strong-armed woman I may never see again. Popsicle juice streams down my hand and I feel like a five-year-old again struggling for the right words, any words. Even before I have them, I open my mouth and lean forward, not yet sure what will spill, my own chopstick fingers thrumming like mad.

Grooming

You are a meticulous groomer. Every morning you crouch under the showerhead for eighteen minutes, spray of hot water baptizing you as you untangle the Old Spice soap-on-a-rope from the hot water faucet handle, your father's scent. A nostalgic indulgence that is getting harder and harder for your wife to procure and wrap up every Christmas, or so she claims. You wonder if she has stockpiled. Found a rich supply the year you married and has been doling them out ever since. She is a faithful woman.

You stroke a plush washcloth against the Old Spice, like rubbing a magic lamp that conjures your father's presence, though he was never really present, always out saving someone else's life. Pulling mothers and babies from burning houses. Dousing flames, windows shattering, embers flying, smoke seeping into his hair, his skin. Such a noble profession. Which explains the Old Spice, the only balm that eradicated the smell. You close your eyes and pretend he is shaving at your sink, performing his own morning ablution while in the kitchen your mother makes oatmeal and slices oranges and stirs extra milk and sugar into your father's hot tea. You can hear her yelling at you: "Hurry up in there, Cal!"

You scuff the washcloth down your arms and legs, leaner now without the muscle of youth, a much flatter behind, ankles as skinny as a girl's. Shampoo twice with Head & Shoulders, groaning at the tangle of hairs slipping toward the drain, so few left now and you imagine that the abundance of foam whipping up in your fingers is your original coif, your locks once so full and lush barbers sighed when you plunked into their chairs.

You rinse, massage the soap from your underarms and crotch, more hairs sloughing off along with dead skin and your vigor. The faucets turn off easily, no straining today since you replaced the rubber washers yesterday. Your faithful wife's complaint. She can't sleep with the unrelenting splat though you never hear it. You doze like a child. Innocent as a lamb. She, however, grunts and grinds molars and tangles sheets with her frigid feet because she brings her work home. All her clients' emotional baggage rammed into her skull along with recipes and the grandkids' birthdays and the hiding place for those medallions of Old Spice. You wonder what secrets your wife has tucked away along with the soap, what wounds her clients reveal, what tragic pasts that she cannot divulge, though you have wheedled and pried because it doesn't feel right that she keeps things from you, even if those things do not belong to her.

The bath rug is plush, the heartbreaking tickle of silky fibers on the soles of your feet as you dry off with an oversized towel. Another insistence. No thin, rough terrycloth for you. You pack your own towels on vacations because hotel towels are like sandpaper against your delicate skin. The family joke. You're so thin-skinned you never could wear starched collars or wool slacks. *Sweet Pea*, your father called you. *Ought to send you to the army and see what military cots feel like.* You know something about army cots though you never enlisted.

You wrap the towel around your waist and squeegee steam from the mirror with the side of your hand, glass squealing as you then swipe the slick surface with the end of a towel so you can examine your torso, count the moles on your chest, create constellations with freckles and skin tags. Stalking lion. Howling wolf. A universe expanding year by year on your pasty skin. You suck in your belly and turn sideways to gauge girth, only slightly thicker than when you played high school football. A swift running back with nimble fingers and *the grace of a panther*, Coach Simpson said. *You are a perfect specimen*, Coach said. To him you were neither soft nor delicate. You were lithe and virile and the most promising athlete he'd seen in years. *Decades*, he said, and you believed him. How you ached to believe him. So did the other players who resented you for it, the special attention, particularly when you got the girl: the perfect unplucked high school sweetheart who could barely look you in the eyes. Your alliterative wife, Connie. Cal and Connie Corbin. You used to attend high school reunions: tenth, twentieth, twenty-fifth, spending months in advance doing sit-ups, lifting barbells. How you appraised your pot-bellied teammates who had gone all doughy, particularly the linebackers. *Sweet Peas*, you wanted to call them. And maybe would have after a few more reunions until Andy Barth with his humorless humor. Gripping your shoulders, smothering you in all that fat, your face in his armpit. Him smelling like fried grease and pungent B.O., introducing you to his third wife as *Dr. and Mrs. Corbin*. You being the *Mrs.* since your wife holds the Ph.D., a title you still can't quite wrap your mouth around. *How's it feel being a kept woman?* Andy taunted at the last reunion you ever attended in 1975. That was ten years ago when all the other wives were still cooking pot roasts and baking homemade pies while you were heating up TV dinners.

You re-wipe the mirror and finally look square at your face, older than you imagine. Every single time you are stunned by those sagging jowls, the puffy under eyes, skin so pale it's nearly translucent.

Though at fifty-five, not at death's door. Unmoored, is the word your Engine Company No. 6 buddies use. All those retired firemen who gather on Saturday mornings at the Waffle House for coffee and bear claws. How they pine for those adrenaline-gushing alarms, those heart-thumping, siren-soaked rides and you miss them, too, because you followed in your father's footsteps. You also climbed ladders to pull mothers and babies from burning houses, ran into engulfed apartment buildings searching for tenants, sweating in your gear, muscles straining under the weight of it all. Such an incongruous occupation given your innate need for cleanliness. But the Waffle House men dipping their donuts are sixty-five, seventy, much older than you, the baby at the table because of your disability. Your last fire ever when the ceiling collapsed, snapping your legs like brittle twigs. *Lucky for you your wife works*, they said when you closed your locker for good.

You squirt a dollop of Barbasol onto the tips of your fingers and slather it onto your cheeks and neck, craning your head this way and that, squinting at the row of six lights over the vanity, 100-watt bulbs so your wife can see to do her makeup. Luminescence you don't need because after all these years you have mapped your cheekbones, jaw, cleft chin, Adam's apple with the precision of a cartographer.

You rinse your hands and pick up the razor. How you hate the cool feel of the blades against your flesh, detest the scraping sound it makes as it rasps down your cheek. Sandpaper. So you shave quickly, methodically, sliding the razor from sideburn to chin in incremental swatches so you don't miss a single hair. Because even if you hate the feel, the sound, you must have a smooth face that won't scratch, won't mar tender skin should you offer a slight kiss, a brush of lips against a velvety cheek. Between strokes you submerge the razor in a sink filled with hot water and tap it against the bottom, watch the cloud of foam and stubble float to the surface. Each day a new Rorschach. *Yes,*

Connie, I know what they are. You try to interpret them: meringue pies your mother used to make; boyhood snow-banks steep enough to sled down; rumple of itchy white sheets on an army cot in a supply closet; tumble of starched shirt on a cold tile floor.

You wonder what white ink blots your father made, if that memory of standing chin high by the sink watching him shave is real or concocted, because you need a memory or two, regardless. Did you really bolster the nerve that chilly morning and ask him to teach you to shave? Did he really say yes and haul in a stool from the kitchen, drape a hand towel over your chest like a bib and slather your face with shaving foam he whipped up in a mug, let you use the back of his comb as a pretend razor so you could copy every stroke, tapping the fake razor in the bottom of a water-filled sink? Or did he in fact say *Not now*, meaning, ultimately, not ever.

At the sink, you unplug the stopper and let the cloudy dream-water gurgle down the pipes before twisting the hot water knob on. You wait for the steam to rise before holding a washcloth underneath, let the fabric soak in the heat before holding it to your face to wipe off excess shaving cream and open those pores so that after the coarse shaving you can slather on the Keri lotion that makes your skin shine. You love the slick cream on your fingers, the tacky feel as you coat your cheeks and neck. The clean smell that doubles as aftershave because after all that Old Spice and Head & Shoulders you don't want to overpower anyone. Subtlety is your preference. You imagine yourself walking by some sullen girl sitting on a park bench, eyes on a pile of leaves at her feet. She hears only your footsteps, feels the air whirling in your wake, smells the hint of lotion, clean and innocent as a newborn. She will lift her chin and moon over your retreating figure which you are certain is not threatening in the least.

You pick up the black comb from the sink and rake it across your hair, the plastic teeth raising welts on your scalp because you refuse to reduce pressure, so little resistance to plow through now. Once the hairs are flattened, you shape waves in the remnants to form a wispy outline of the pompadour you sported in your glory days. And then the routine you hide even from your wife—because if she can have secrets, so can you—you grab her unscented hairspray and offer a few pumps to secure your efforts.

The phone rings and you flinch. You should race to the bedside table before the phone screams again and disturbs your dozing wife, but you don't, because it's undoubtedly for her. The office. A client's mental meltdown, yet again. More rescuing, more secrets to keep, giving you less and less to discuss at the dinner table on those nights when she is home.

At times you wish you had been more forceful in squelching her college-bound plan. The children were in high school and didn't need her anymore, she claimed. How you fiddled with your leather watchband and warned her that it would be hard going, she would probably quit, and that would be okay because you loved her that much. Still needed her that much. But she didn't drop out and now her practice is thriving. She is a different woman than the spindly eighteen-year-old you carried across the threshold. As ignorant as a peach. She's not ignorant now, but neither are you, she always insists at those fancy dinner parties and cocktail hours where she has received so many accolades. *And what do you do?* guests ask when they pump your hand. *He's a voracious reader,* Connie offers, which is the truth. You read Dostoyevsky and Joyce in high school. *But what's your line of work?* those suit-clad guests probe so they will know how to rank you, at least that's how you always felt. *He was a fireman,* your wife says. She blathers on about your heroics, listing your awards, your accolades. And there have been plenty. You have had trees planted in your name, park benches installed by grateful families. *But what do you do now?* they prod. *I'm on disability,* you answer, and it's nothing to be ashamed of you assure yourself as your wife slips away through the crowd. You pretend she is not wearing your father's exact expression every time he glared at your legs that could no longer bear the weight of fighting fires.

Which is why you started tutoring at the high school, because you had to do something. Not at the same school you attended, but the sprawling, consolidated version that pulled together your school and your rival's across town. But the kids don't mind, not anymore, since they have new adversaries to worry about. When the school opened officials pleaded for volunteers to help tutor lagging children in reading and math. Particularly the jocks. You felt the urge and didn't even bother to ask your wife if it was a good idea. When was the last time she bothered to ask you anything?

That first day you shaved extra close, the sandpaper excruciating but you endured it because this was important. Your first big impression. You chose your dress wisely, soft sweater and slacks, and wound your way through the labyrinthine halls toward the football coach's office, such an odd feeling in your gut. He was pleasant enough, Coach Boggs, no scratchy five o'clock shadow that Coach Simpson sported even in the morning. This new coach wore tidy Dockers and a Polo shirt. No whistle around his neck. No supply closet behind him with a narrow cot for catnaps. No bathroom of his own with the metal paper towel dispenser, those coarse, brown paper sheets that nearly rubbed you raw.

And then the cutting news that where you were really needed with your well-read history was in the library. The apparent dismay on your closely-shaven face. You slogged down the hall feeling demoted until Miss Wallace, the antiquated librarian who could barely see, rose to clasp your hand and usher you to a carrel in the back corner where your first pupil waited. And there she sat, Brenda, a sloop-shouldered girl who barely peeled her eyes from her shoes, anxious for you to open up to her the world of books.

But she opened up to you, too. It was an accident, really. *Great Expectations*, poor Pip, and how chapter by chapter, week by week, Brenda discovered how cruel adults can be to children, even fictitious ones. How finally one day tears rimmed Brenda's eyes and you surprised even yourself by confessing your own inner wounds. That's all Brenda needed, that small door opening and she walked right through it. All tears and hiccups and bangs in her eyes, her head on your shoulder, hand on your wrist, your fingers stroking her silky hair. So excruciatingly soft.

Today you tiptoe to the closet to select just the right ensemble. The cashmere sweater your wife bought you that brings out the green in your eyes. The brown slacks and argyle socks and polished shoes. You spot a scuff on the toe and pull the shoe polish kit from the bathroom closet and sit on the closed toilet seat to buff it out. Perfect, but now your hands are stained and you wash them thoroughly in the sink, dry them completely before applying more Keri. Your hands have to be soft, for Jenny. Not Brenda anymore, who graduated years ago. Not Nancy or Linda or Dawn. All gone off to college with scholarships in hand thanks to you. Your tutoring, your encouragement, your praise because you have it down. Your initial shyness as you ascertain her demeanor because she has to be just right. As innocent as a peach. And by now you know the signs. If she hides behind long hair or baggy clothes. If she can't at first look directly at you. If her voice is as soft as an echo so she won't draw attention, and when she finally looks into your eyes, and you squint into hers, your heart thunks when you spot the elusive shadow, the vulnerability and fear. And then you know. You can begin using a cooing voice the first few weeks. Hand pats after that when she doesn't stumble so much over elaborate words, jumbled syllables. Then your arm around her shoulder with a *Job well done.* Which deserves a reward. A milkshake at Sonic Drive-In so you can sit in your car with such a small space between you, just like your courting days with Connie at Twilight's before they tore it down. You angle the rearview mirror up sharply to block out brutal reminders. You can pretend once again you are a swift running back with the grace of a panther, such a perfect specimen.

Weeks later, if it's warm, you'll drive to North End Park where nobody goes. You will find a bench under a shady, shadowy tree and tell her how special she is, your best pupil by far. And she will believe you. How she'll ache to believe you. *Such deep thoughts,* you will say. *Such maturity for one so young.* She will feel chosen, and she is, so now you can slip your hand around her waist and pull her to you. Your hip against hers as you sit closer and closer. She'll whiff the sweet blend of Old Spice and Keri. But that's enough for one day. You slide your fingers through her hair as a parting good-bye. A fleeting kiss on the cheek. The next week you will brush your lips briefly against hers, an uncle, a brother, a mentor. But of course you are much more than that, and she knows it. A morsel that makes her flush with pride.

After that the best week of all, the intervening days when the anticipation puts a lift in your step. A chirp in your voice. A warm ball in your chest flooding you with light. You are not impatient because the adrenaline is as exquisite as bursting out of a blazing house to deliver a rescued toddler into the arms of her mother. Such sweet salvation.

Which brings you to today. The soft sweater. Soft hands. Your wife sleeping after re-cradling the phone, eyelids fluttering as her mind whips her patients' pasts into a distorted carnival. You do not disturb her. She can have it all.

Because Jenny waits like a wispy field of unplowed wheat, all beige and silky. Her mouth a plump nectarine, perfectly ripe, and today you will press your lips against hers and hold it. Just hold it. Her initial alarm buckling under the trust you have built, such a sturdy, painstaking façade. Worth every hour, every week, every month because there is nothing better than the instant you slide your tongue between her lips and the magic happens. The delectable moment when she gives it all over and you hold her tragic secret in your mouth like a precious, glowing gem.

Amnesty

As soon as I rounded the corner I knew, sweet Jesus, someone was free!

Uncle Paolo was bent under the old Buick's hood.

"Who is it?" I said, running up the gravel driveway spraying stones. "Who is out?"

Uncle Paolo straightened, wiped his hands on a greasy rag, and slammed the hood down. "Load the valises, Ana. I am getting too old for this."

Three suitcases sat beside the opened trunk: Uncle Paolo's, Uncle Eliseo's, and Uncle Luis's. I hoisted them inside with a grunt and turned back to Paolo, who was clomping up the front porch steps toward the screen door.

Air in the house was thick with anticipation. The three children sat in a fidgety row on the sofa, a chocolate-dipped banana in each hand to keep them quiet. Pocked María knelt before them with two fingers poised for horns as she told them the story of Ramon the bull.

She turned when I entered behind Uncle Paolo and I mouthed the word, "Who?" María scrunched up her face and shrugged before charging the children who squealed in mock terror.

In the yellow-tiled kitchen Fat Carmelita stacked bean and avocado tortillas for the uncles to eat on the trip.

"Who?" I said before putting down my purse or peeling off my cleaning smock from work.

She looked at me with both onion and happy tears in her eyes. "Hector," she said. "He is free!"

I crossed myself and kissed my thumb up to heaven.

"Ave María," I said. Hector. My dead husband's cousin. He stayed with me after they stole my Felipe, and once again the other time, the even worse time.

Fat Carmelita went back to her beans.

"How?" I asked.

"How should I know? The uncles never tell us anything." She slapped down a spoonful of beans. "But we got a call today from Guatemala City."

"Guatemala City!"

Carmelita looked over her shoulder at me and pointed her spoon. "You know. I think it was that Emilio Vega. I'll never forget how beautiful he was."

"Yes," I said. "Very beautiful. But not as pretty as my Felipe."

"Oh no," she said, not to be out-mourned. "Not nearly as handsome as my Manuel."

Soon we loaded the uncles down with lunch bags and root beer and the special jar because of Uncle Luis's weak bladder. They left after kissing our cheeks and patting each child's head.

"We'll be back tomorrow," Uncle Paolo yelled from the car. "Find a place for Hector to sleep."

Sleep. Ah. Where would our dear Hector sleep? He would be number ten in our household of threes. Three men. Three women. Three children. I always felt especially blest in our trinity house. As if we had a unique bond with the Father, Son, and Holy Ghost. Carmelita called us a family of mismatched socks. No sister had a brother. No father had a daughter. No child had a parent.

And now we had to squeeze in one more. We women paraded through the house, followed by a tangle of children, and Gringa, the little white dog. We measured closets and corners, window seats and floor space, but nothing would do. Finally I stopped in front of the one door behind which I knew there was plenty of room. I flung the door open wide. The candles inside wavered, and the children sucked in their breath at the blasphemy.

I scanned the alcove with the candelabras and crosses, holy water fonts just inside the door. Along one wall sat the burgundy sofa with the propped-up left leg. On the opposite wall above the flickering candles were thumbtacked pictures of those who had been disappeared for saying *No!* or saying nothing at all. Our fathers, mothers, husbands, wives. Even our children. We knew the fates of some, but not all. On the highest row, the one nearest God, were the faces of those we knew to be dead. In the middle of this row, between the two tiny photos that for the longest time I could not bear to look at, was my husband Felipe with his beautiful white-toothed grin.

Ah, that grin. On our wedding night I told Felipe the only reason I married him was because of his teeth. It is true. Good teeth, good bones. I wanted sturdy children from this man. Before he turned out the light he leaned close to my ear and whispered, "You'll get more than that from me, Sweetness."

And he was right. But so was I. We did make beautiful babies.

"No-No-No!" Carmelita said, jolting me out of my reverie. "To use this room would be a sacrilege. This is where we pray for our lost souls."

"Ana," Pocked María whispered, "This is God's room."

"God doesn't need his own room," I said. "And even if he does, I'm sure he would share it with Hector."

The children looked from one of us to the other until Carmelita said, "Well, there is a perfectly good sofa if we throw on a blanket."

Pocked María said, "Maybe a hook or two in the wall for his clothes?"

So it was settled.

The next morning Carmelita began filling every bowl in her kitchen with her most special recipes. The ones she wouldn't give to anyone, not even Mrs. Fina, who owned the best taqueria in town.

Pocked María scrubbed the children so hard they cried. No sharing bath water this time either. Each got a fresh tub and a warm pan dulce from Carmelita's kitchen if they promised to stay clean.

Me, I went shopping with my money from work. It's just dusting and vacuuming at Widow Greenbaum's gallery, but you would have thought I wanted to join the priesthood the way the uncles fussed.

"Why do you need to work, Ana?" Luis said. "There's plenty of cleaning to be done at home." He turned to Eliseo. "Aye. She is becoming like these American women. Too independent."

Paolo snapped his grimy, red suspenders. "Wouldn't you prefer to marry again, Ana? It has been seven years since Felipe. Mango on the corner has expressed interest, and you are not too old to bear."

To bear! He thought this would entice me? To bear? I no longer had the optimism for such things. I already had my husband, my children, that part of my life. What else was I to do if not work? Besides, I had already asked Felipe's permission, and he nodded assent, though I dared not bring this up to the uncles.

You see, though I was born with the strength of the Martinez women, when I first found out Felipe was dead my courage climbed into a deep hole. It was dark and cold and I swear my breath came out in white puffs. I often sat shivering on the burgundy sofa burrowing deeper into that pit.

Then I had the vision, and no it wasn't because I hadn't slept for six days as the uncles liked to believe. I was crying in the alcove, eyes locked shut, when I heard "Ana." I opened my eyes and there was Felipe, leaning out of his picture as if it were a window frame. He held out a black and white hand.

"I am here," he said, pulling my hand to his lips for a kiss that was as soft as I remembered. "Do not worry. I am watching," he said, and a spray of childish giggles erupted. I stole a peek at first one twin, then the other, and shut my eyes fast.

So I still had my family, and I would busy my days with cycles of work and sleep. Work and sleep, until the day I would finally join them.

But how could I explain this to the uncles?

"The children need new shoes," I said to them. "You want the neighbors thinking we are only backward farmers who cannot afford to buy our children shoes?" I knew this appeal to their machismo would work. And so five days a week I donned a blue apron and trotted off to the gallery. My only endurance was passing Mango's nursery. Whenever he saw me he tipped his straw hat and waved his fertilizer-encrusted hand. "You put my tulips to shame," he would say, or carnations, daffodils, whatever he happened to be tending. Though I liked the compliment, something inside made me quicken my pace and gather my smock in front to hide my ovaries. I knew Felipe would scowl at this attention, but who can deny a husband's jealousy?

Still, it was worth it to have my own money so I could buy the personal items Hector would need: comb, razor, toothbrush, scapula for protection. I slid into the alcove clutching the crinkled Wal-Mart bag. A soft afghan covered the couch, and a TV tray stood against one wall. A hand mirror hung above it from a nail. I laid Hector's toiletries in a neat row on the tray and sat on the sofa to search the walls for Hector's face. There he was, third row from the bottom, next to

Patricia, his wife. "Today one of you is coming to life," I said, rising to take down his image. "This will give you courage," I said, examining the creamy rectangle behind Hector's picture that had been hiding from the candles' sooty flames. "Maybe you can push through these walls too," I said to the faces. To Elena, Alberto, José. I stood on tiptoes to hold Hector's picture up to Felipe. "Look who is coming home today." I kissed my finger and touched it to my husband's lips, and quickly did it twice more for the twins.

Then Hector came.

Two faces peered from each window after Pocked María yelled, "Here they are!" The Buick eased carefully into the driveway, as if Uncle Paolo suddenly remembered a carton of eggs he'd left up on top. When they stopped, three doors popped open, and the uncles disembarked to scurry to the fourth. Uncle Eliseo got there first, opened the door, and reached his hands deep inside. Uncle Luis grabbed Eliseo's hips from behind to add strength, but he needn't have bothered, because the form Eliseo withdrew was so thin and brittle. Fat Carmelita said, "Sweet Jesus, Ana. He walks like an old-old man. Like Don Migalito with his popping knees."

We gathered in the living room prepared with smiles and embraces. María warned the children, but we were still afraid they would rush and cling to Hector begging sweets. But when he finally came into the house, so stooped and narrow, the brightness slid from the children's faces. They ran to the kitchen to hide behind Fat Carmelita, who remembered just in time about the flan before it burned.

I wanted to hide behind her apron, too, but I made myself stay and look at Hector though it hurt my eyes to do it. To see so many scars like shiny purple worms crawling out of his collar and up his neck. Half of his right ear was missing, and the eye on that side roamed freely, unseeing, disconnected from the left.

Hector would not meet our gaze with his. We weren't even sure if he was aware of our presence. At one time each of us had stood in Hector's shoes, the one getting out, and we knew that, for Hector, none of this was quite real. Still, we tried to hug him, welcome him. But no warmth emitted from his skin to say, I accept your kindness. I am happy to be here.

We stood shuffling feet, clearing throats, saying things like, "Well," and "How was the trip," and "Yes, those armadillos are muy estupi-dos!" All the while Hector stared at the floor, slumped forward, like the fluid that once stretched his skin taut had been drained. Finally Uncle Paolo had the wisdom to say, "This is no time for a fiesta. What Hector needs is sleep."

Everyone gratefully agreed, and when I led them to the alcove, Uncle Eliseo smoothed the ripple of my fear when he said, "It is good. It would not do to have the household running on top of him just now." We led him to the couch, and Uncle Luis pushed on Hector's collar bone so he would sit, which he did, with his knees pressed tight together and his arms at his sides.

This was how I found him when I brought his evening tray. Candles flickered in the breeze of my entrance. I saw their reflection in the hand mirror, but not in Hector's waxy eyes. The only thing I could think to do was nudge his shoulder so he might lie down. In one stiff movement he tipped over, but still with his body pressed into a tight Z. I angled him more evenly on the sofa and covered him for sleep.

For four days he slept just like that. No one dared to wake him, though we wanted to hug him, and cry for him, and rub on the jojoba salve Aunt Tulia sent all the way from Amarillo—Federal Express—and you know that wasn't cheap! Not even the dog went near Hector, and she begged scraps from anyone.

When I returned from work each day I asked María, "Did he move?"

"No."

"Is he still breathing?"

"Yes."

"This can't be good for his kidneys."

"No, but what would you have us do?"

I didn't know, so finally I asked Carmelita, "Should we wake him?"

"I don't know," she said. "But he must take liquids soon."

"Yes." I reached in the cabinet for the tallest glass and filled it with water.

"Wait," Carmelita said, and stirred in a spoonful of honey. "It's something, at least."

I carried the glass like an offering, followed by Carmelita, who wiped her hands on an apron though there was no need. For the first time since Hector's arrival I noticed how quiet the house was. "Where are the children?" I said. And when I saw Hector's untouched lunch tray, "And Gringa the dog?"

"María keeps them outside all day," Carmelita said. "Every time the children come in they remember about Hector and hide. Lupé even got his head caught under the kitchen sink."

Cousin Hector still had not moved, so I knelt beside him. Palming his shoulder I gave a nudge so slight I wasn't even sure I'd done it, but Hector's eyes popped open like he'd been waiting for someone to do just that. He still did not meet his good eye with ours, but when I slipped my hand behind his back to raise him, he did not resist. And when I held the glass to his lips, he drank. I turned to smile at Carmelita, but she had already rushed to the kitchen to heat up chicken broth.

So began Hector's slow conformation to the patterns of the house. Sleep when it is dark. Awake when it is light. During the day he sat rigid on his sofa, rising only to go to the bathroom with the uncles' assistance. Everyday we took turns sweet-talking and coaxing.

"Would you like to go outside, Hector? To the movies? En Español. How about some ice cream?" Hector would not go outside, but eventually he did take meals with the family, though he ate very little, and always slipped a buttered tortilla into his pants pocket to hide under his sofa. Pocked María scooped them out each morning when he left the room, but no one had the heart to tell him to stop, not even the uncles, who thought wasting food was a venial sin at least.

The children grew accustomed to this new uncle. They no longer hid, and even crouched outside his door sliding metal cars and plastic dolls across the floor into his foot to see if he would move, say a word, blink. I scolded when I found them, but not until the last toy slid, because I hoped their game would work.

And one day it did, which scattered the children back into hiding, and made me freeze in an awkward position. When the ceramic burro hit his foot, Hector tilted his head down and watched it skid across the floor and rest under the candelabras. He rose and walked toward it, no longer with don Migalito's popping knees, more like a shuffle, as if the weight of each foot was just too much. He bent to retrieve the blue burro, and a red Matchbox car, a rubber dog bone, a Barbie leg, and held them to his chest and stood face to face with all those pictures he had not seen before. Clutching the toys to his concave belly with one hand, he traced the grid between the pictures with the other, careful not to touch one shiny edge. Underneath each photo his finger paused. I waited to see what he would do at Patricia, but his pause was no longer or shorter for her than for anyone else. I thought, *He does not know!*

When I brought this up to the uncles, Paolo twisted the worn gold band on his thick finger and said, "You think he is ready to work?"

Luis cleared his throat and said, "Yes, now maybe he is."

"Uncles," I said. "Didn't you hear me? I don't think Cousin Hector knows about his disappeared wife!"

I looked at the uncles and there was an unbearable pause when their eyes bruised back to the moment when they realized their own horrible losses. Then suddenly, almost in unison, they shook it off and Uncle Paolo said, "He may not even remember he *had* a wife. Does that mean he cannot push a broom? I am sixty-seven and I push a broom."

I dropped my arms to my sides with a smack. How did they think Hector could push a broom? He barely left his alcove, which worried me because he was turning the color of Mr. Velázquez's cataracts.

"Uncles," I said, forcing calm. "Let me tend to him awhile longer. Take him outside in the sun. Work his muscles so he can push a *big* broom for you. Maybe even run heavy machinery."

The uncles rubbed their scratchy beards, nodding, until Uncle Eliseo said, "Yes, he will work better once his body is built back. Not like us," he indicated their three sagging, purple-veined bodies. "It will be good to have a strong man working for the house."

Now each afternoon before removing my smock, I inserted my arm into Hector's like a key and pulled him outside. It was difficult at first. He had to shield his eyes from the sun, and his weighted feet scraped noisily across the ground. But our circuit grew daily, from the porch, to the mailbox, to the street sign on the corner, even to Mango's tipping, straw hat.

When Hector wasn't walking he stared at the alcove walls. At the pictures, I mean, for hours and hours. Every time I peeked in to say Good night, Hector; Good morning, Hector; Time for our walk; he was standing there, facing the walls, with his arms at his sides, looking. He even moved the candelabras so he could stare up close.

"That's something," Carmelita once said, tapping her head. "It shows that even if he isn't talking, he's thinking up there."

And I guess he was, because one evening I saw him nose-to-nose with his Patricia. He even pressed his forehead against her glossy finish.

At night, in bed, while the household slept, I could feel Felipe's arms around me, his warm breath on my neck. I would wait for Carmelita to snore like a creaking mattress spring and then, in my lowest voice, I would tell my husband the events of the day: Lupé lost a tooth; Uncle Luis backed into the fire hydrant again; Hector polished his shoes with just a little help from me. One night Felipe squeezed me tight and said, "That's good, Ana. But don't forget that I need you, that your children need you, too."

"Never," I said. "I could never forget that."

Then he stroked my hair until I, too, snored like a creaking spring.

On a Sunday in May Hector and I walked my route to the gallery. It was only a destination; we hadn't meant to go inside. But sitting on the doorstep was Widow Greenbaum, her head wrapped in the orange scarf she always wore. She had a pickle in her mouth and was drawing on the sidewalk—right on concrete!

She withdrew the pickle as we approached. "Look who is coming to visit on such a pretty day," she said. It wasn't always easy to understand her. Learning English was difficult enough, but hearing it strained through a Polish tongue was most frustrating.

"Ana!" she said, rising to greet me. "I was just—" She stopped when she saw Hector and the pickle fell right out of her hand, hitting the sidewalk with a dull thwack. Then she stepped right past me and stood before Hector.

"Poor angel," she said. "What have they done to you?" She cupped his face in her tiny Polish hands. Hector only stared straight ahead and let her do it. Then she pulled a hanky from her sleeve and loudly blew her nose. From the other sleeve she produced a Snickers bar and handed it to Hector, who promptly slid it inside his shirt.

"I'm sorry," I said. "He does the same at home."

"Don't apologize, Ana," she said. "*This* I understand. Now come inside and let me feed you." She took Hector's wrist and poked a finger into his belly. "Such skin-and-bones," she said, and led him into the gallery.

I'm no artist, but I could never comprehend the paintings hanging on those walls. Giant naked ladies with green faces and purple breasts. Men with huge feet and tiny heads—no fig leafs there! One painting was totally black. I swear on my dead mother's braid it was two meters by two meters of nothing but black. But hey, like I said, I'm no artist.

Widow Greenbaum sat Hector on a stool by the rhododendron. "I have some nice Gouda and a tin of sardines," she said. "Oh! And somewhere there is a box of shortbread cookies." She scurried to the kitchenette and Hector popped right off his stool and went for those paintings. He stood in front of one I bet five minutes. Five minutes to look at blue and yellow blobs. Finally I joined him and craned my neck. "What is it you see in there, Hector?" He kept on staring just like at the pictures at home. Blue and yellow blobs. That's all.

Widow Greenbaum returned with a cheese- and fruit-laden tray. "Ah," she said. "It's one of my favorites, too."

Then Hector moved to a different painting. Purple streaks with green, the paint all mixed together as if the artist couldn't be bothered to clean his brush. But Hector inspected it as intently as the first.

It was difficult to pull him away from the gallery.

"Come again anytime," Widow Greenbaum yelled to Hector as we hurried off toward home.

I guess the uncles were impressed with Hector's progress, because one night I found a folded section of newspaper beside the toilet. Uncle Paolo left his reading material behind. I only meant to retrieve it, but the red circles made me read: WANTED: MANUAL LABORER. NO SPECIAL SKILLS. DUTIES INCLUDE HEAVY

LIFTING; WANTED: COOK. NO EXP. NECC. BENITO'S BUR-
RITOS; WANTED: BOUNCER. HOURS 9 P.M. - 2 A.M. EVE'S
EDEN. The last one scared me so much I had bad dreams that
night. They all involved Hector flipping burgers at a—I'm too embarrassed to say where.

When I was leaving for work the next morning, Hector got up
from his couch, without prodding, and put on his coat. I said, "No
Hector, this is not our walk. I have to go to work. Trabajar." As I
closed the door behind me I felt bad, but what could I do? It wasn't
until Mango's nursery that I recognized Hector's scraping. And sure
enough, when I turned around, there he was, heading toward me.
"No Hector," I said, "Work!" But he wouldn't stop, and really, I was so
proud of his initiative I didn't have the heart to send him back. Even
Mango tipped his hat and said, "He's looking much better these days,
Ana. But I would too under your care."

When we got to the gallery I sat him on the stool and told him,
"Stay," just like I might tell Gringa the dog.

Of course you know he did not stay. He went right to those paintings. I shook my head and said, "Okay, but don't touch," and went off
to find Widow Greenbaum.

She was sitting on a stool on top of a rickety table in the studio,
her pant legs rolled up to her knees. Seven students sat or stood behind wooden easels frantically sketching Widow Greenbaum's feet,
her toenails painted shiny as red Christmas balls.

"Two minutes," she said to the students, and then she saw me
peering in the doorway. "Yes, Ana."

The students swiveled toward me, but immediately returned to
their drawings.

"It's Hector," I whispered, pointing back to the gallery. "He's
with me."

"It's good," she said. "It was for him I made this gallery."

I nodded, puzzled, and backed into the hall.

From then on Hector accompanied me to work. The uncles weren't pleased, but I told them it was practice for when he got a job of his own. And really, it was like his work. Each day Hector moved from painting to painting, staring sometimes seven minutes without blinking—I know because I timed it.

You'd think his legs would tire after so much standing, but they didn't, I guess, because as soon as we got home he headed straight for his alcove to resume the staring. Only this time it was into a wall crowded with faces. Sometimes the uncles peered in, shook their heads, and shuffled back down the hall.

A few weeks later while I was scrubbing the gallery's kitchenette Widow Greenbaum hollered from the studio, "Ana, please bring me a hanger from the cloak room."

I hated going into the studio while the students worked. Something about their scrunched faces made me nervous. I was glad when Hector followed, though he stood just outside the door. He wouldn't go in where the pupils were noisily setting up sketch pads and tool boxes. Widow Greenbaum was talking, hands flapping, to a woman I'd never seen. She was swathed from neck to ankles in peach cloth. Her skin was the color of cocoa powder from the can. I thought surely if I blew across her cheek she would swirl away.

Widow Greenbaum motioned me toward them. "Ana," she said, "this is our new model, Maranga. She speaks very little English." I nodded and she smiled. Then she looked at Widow Greenbaum who nodded as well.

Maranga turned away from us, untucked one end of her wrap, and it fell noiselessly to the floor. When she turned back around I noticed the taut skin over her stomach which was ripe with a child. She tried to bend and retrieve her wrap, but couldn't, so she let out a laugh that was smooth, like water sliding over pebbles.

I stooped to collect the peach fabric and hung it carefully over the hanger.

Aqua blue fabric was nailed to the ceiling, spilled down the wall and across the floor. Widow Greenbaum led Maranga to a stool in the middle of all that color. *Madonna*, I thought, and tried to move, but I couldn't stop marveling at the beauty of this woman. The yellow-rose color of the palms of her hands, the soles of her feet. The white shine on the bulge of her stomach. Hector was watching, too, with his head tilted down, but his eyes aimed up. Widow Greenbaum slowly circled Maranga, pushing a shoulder, arranging a hand. "May I?" she asked before touching her stomach. Maranga smiled and nodded. Widow Greenbaum placed her hands on each side and began to gently feel the shape. "Beautiful," she said, and I felt a twinge in my own belly, or an ache. Suddenly I felt like a bitter wind could blow clean through me. I grabbed Hector's wrist and tried to pull him away but he wouldn't move. "Come on, Hector," I said, "We mustn't disturb them." *Still* he would not budge. "Hector!" I said, then Maranga said something I didn't understand. Widow Greenbaum translated, "She says he may stay if he likes." So I dropped Hector's arm and left them to their work while I attended to mine.

That night, without thinking, I slid a folded pillow under the covers until it rested on my flat belly. Then I caressed the soft mound, whispering, "Shh, shh," until I drifted off to sleep.

Hector now spent his days sitting on a stool just outside the studio, watching several different versions of Maranga being pulled out of the students' canvases. He still stared for minutes without blinking, sometimes quarters of an hour, but at home he stopped his staring altogether.

Now he paced, back and forth, in front of the wall of faces.

It was a nervous kind of pacing, as if any minute he might break into a run. It reminded me of Loco Lindy, my dead father's unbreakable mare. One minute she would be nibbling tender green shoots. The next she would gallop across the field pitching dirt clods behind her.

The uncles took this as a sign that Hector was ready for work at last.

"Uncles," I said, "he still does not speak."

"He is ready, Ana," Uncle Luis said, and one more thing I wasn't expecting, "and soon you will be able to quit that cleaning job and stay home where you belong."

I could tell by three stern pairs of eyebrows that their minds were made up.

What was I to do with no job? Stay home and pick up crayons and cigar butts? Scoop up little dog turds from the yard? It wasn't enough to fill up my hollowness. I needed something, anything, to busy my hands, my mind. But to tell you the truth, lately the ache had been growing, or the job had been shrinking. I'm not sure which.

Felipe, what should I do? Suddenly I realized with a cringe that I hadn't asked his advice in quite some time.

I went to the alcove to confer with my spouse. Hector was pacing, as usual, but I felt certain he wouldn't mind the intrusion. I edged as close to the wall as possible to stay out of his path, and told Felipe the bad news. Today, however, he gave me nothing. Not a word. Not a blink.

"Aw, come on Felipe," I said. "Don't be so tight-lipped."

Still he stared straight ahead.

"Maybe you're busy," I finally said. "I'll come back tomorrow."

Which I did, and the next day, and the day after that, but for six days he said nothing.

Stumped, I crossed my arms and stole a glance of the twins. "Your father has been in quite a mood," I said, but their eyes were as vacant as their father's.

I jumped when Pocked María opened the door.

"Sorry," she said. "I was looking for Hector."

"Hector?" I said, scanning the room. I hadn't even noticed his absence. "Try the bathroom?"

"Good idea," she said, and left.

I looked once more at my husband, my children, but they just stared through me like snapshots. Two dimensional, flat-finished. That's all.

I left the alcove and shut the door tight.

María leaned out the front door calling, "Hector! Hector!"

"Not in the bathroom?" I said.

She pulled back in, "No. Or the kitchen. The bedrooms. It's dark outside, Ana. Where could he be?"

"I'll take a look around the yard," I said, slipping past her. Scratching my elbow, I stepped from the porch and walked around the house calling, "Hector! Hector!" Gringa came to me instead, ramming her cold nose into my ankle. I scooped her up and scratched her forehead. "What have you done with our Hector?" I said, her tail thumping against my side. I set the dog down and started walking our route to the gallery. Where else did Hector know to go?

So this was it. Soon there would be no more walks to work. The uncles would put an end to my job, and poor Hector would be tucking flyers under windshield wipers or buffing fenders at the car wash.

Still, it felt good to be out in the warm night under bright stars. I had never taken this route in the dark. I peered in windows at the Gonzales children gathered in their kitchen for a late supper. The father hoisted a toddler into a high chair while his wife flailed a dish towel and yelled. Two houses down, through the screen door, I could see the Medina boys lying belly down on the floor, heads propped on their arms watching TV in the dark. Across the street Spinster Avila sat alone on her sofa crocheting pot holders. On her porch, dozens of wind chimes clinked out soft melodies. Farther down, Mango's lilacs were particularly sweet.

At the gallery I was surprised to find the front door not only unlocked, but wide open. Easing inside the dark room I paused to listen. The moon spilled eerie shadows across the purple-breasted women and I forced out a shaky "¿Hola?"

Nothing.

I walked toward the hall. Widow Greenbaum was sitting on Hector's stool in a florescent beam cast from the studio doorway. She turned at the sound of creaking floorboards and reached out one hand to me while she dabbed a Kleenex to her eyes with the other. I slipped my hand into hers and she squeezed it too tight.

"What's wrong?" I said. She tilted her head toward the studio, directing me to look inside.

Hector.

He knelt on the floor, bent over a canvas. Paint tubes were scattered by his side, the colors spilling, blending right on the linoleum. With his left hand he traced the scars on his neck, up his jaw. The half ear. The dead eye. With his right fingers he scooped up orange, purple, green, whatever colors he sensed were right and slid them onto his painting. His motions were timid, even holy. Widow Greenbaum nodded in silence as if she knew exactly what each dab of black, each magenta streak meant.

It was too much to see. For several minutes all I could do was squeeze my eyes shut and listen to the sliding of paint. When I finally opened my eyes what I saw was Maranga. Not on Hector's canvas, but lining the walls. Dozens of versions of that beautiful cocoa woman, her belly swollen with so much life.

I became aware of a pulse in my own belly. It was a puzzle and I looked at Hector, so calm in his creation, and Widow Greenbaum, who seemed to understand something about this moment I did not.

"I must go," I said with an urgency that surprised me. Widow Greenbaum nodded, but continued to stare at Hector and blot at the corners of her eyes. I doubted if Hector was even aware of my presence.

Pushing outside I looked up into groupings of stars, bright planets, the edge of the moon, the same moon that sliced the Guatemalan sky. For the first time I was remembering my family instead of imagining them. They were swaying on the porch swing Felipe made when I was pregnant. My daughter snuggled at her father's right side clutching her frayed blanket. My son curled at his left, noisily sucking a thumb. Felipe would make up stories about Rosa the goat in a rhythmic voice that would lull his children toward dreams, and suddenly Guatemala seemed much farther away than 2200 miles and seven years.

I found myself standing before Mango's nursery, my face buried deep in his shrubs. Through the front window I could see him pruning a generous spider plant, offering tender apologies before clipping each stem.

I peeled a cluster of lilac and held it to my face to feel the lavender blossoms against my lips and inhale the thick sweetness deep into my lungs.

It was a potion.

And suddenly I could see myself stepping up onto Mango's porch, rapping on the door. Under the yellow bug light his mouth would curve into a smile as I invited him outside for a chat. Then perhaps, if the moment was right, we would sit on *his* porch swing along with my ghosts, and discuss his fertile garden, my green thumb, and trade secrets well into the night.

Distillation

Betty sits in the passenger seat with an aluminum foil swan on her lap. Twisted inside are leftovers of the supper she paid for. She bought Jeff's too, and now he sits behind the wheel, looking out the front window at the ribbon of I-45 South rushing toward him, at mile markers passing, at the thin strip of pink light on the horizon, as his wife slowly wrings the swan's neck.

"I know where you're going," Betty says.

Jeff grips the wheel tighter. "I thought it would give us closure," he says. "Isn't that what this night is about?"

"I don't have time for this, Jeff. I told the sitter I'd be home by nine."

"Sitter-schmitter," he says, trying to grin at her. Trying to act as if he's not worried about the babysitter, about scalding bath water, about sneaked-in, child-molesting boyfriends, about shaken baby syndrome though the baby is three and a half. The grin comes off as a smirk in the car's dim interior and Betty huffs and looks out her side window.

Jeff settles into the beaded seat cover, the same cover he sat on ten years ago when he drove Betty to Texas City that first time. The same car, too, a two-toned Monte Carlo he inherited from his father, with 112,000 miles less on the odometer. Without the Juicy Juice stains on the back seat that spot remover would not, could *not* remove even after Jeff's repeated applications; no sour milk and baby spit smells that still linger though he sprinkled baking soda and vacuumed until every Melba toast crumb, every dried Spaghettio was safely sucked inside the Dust Buster. It was an eager car, then. New tires anxious to eat up mile after mile. Now it's just part of Jeff's settlement along with the microwave; the twenty-inch TV; the alphabetized collection of baseball cards that he decreased in value by laminating, but *how else are you supposed to keep them clean!* Betty is selling the house her geological drafting job paid for. She gets the rest of the furniture, the two-year-old Dodge Caravan, and Stephanie. Betty gets Stephanie.

But tonight Jeff pretends they're driving back through time. He sucks in his gut as if that'll lighten the twenty-three pounds he's gained since the marriage. If he doesn't look at her, he can envision the svelte, pre-baby woman who rode beside him all those years ago. Happy, jittery, elated about her first trip to the Gulf. She had just moved to Houston four months before. Made the long trip from West Virginia all by herself with a baseball bat on the car seat beside her for protection. He remembers turning onto the Texas City dike at twilight, passing Latino fisherman icing down fish, packing up rods and reels. Others just settling into lawn chairs, breaking out po' boy sandwiches and bottles of Corona, metal coolers beside them waiting for their nighttime catch. Jeff parked at the end of the dike and he and Betty got out and sat on the car's hood. *Amazing*, Betty had said, scanning the oil refineries just across the water, an Erector Set city of gridwork outlined by millions of lights, flare stacks shooting flames. *It's like Christmas*, she had said. Jeff pointed out cooling towers, transformers, catalytic cracking units—cat crackers, he called them, and distillation columns, the largest structures of all, some over two-hundred feet high. *How do you know all their names?* Betty asked. *I worked here one summer,* he said, neglecting to mention that he got fired his first week for spending six hours meticulously painting a railing that his boss said should have taken thirty minutes. Jeff said that though you couldn't see them, there were probably men out there climbing stairways around columns, or clanking up catwalks in steel-toed boots, troubleshooting, making sure everything was smoothly running. *Climbing in the dark?* Betty asked, eyes straining to make out tiny silhouettes against the lights. *They must be brave,* she said. Jeff remembers the look of utter awe on her face. Admiration. *It's nothing,* he said. *I did it a million times.*

"It got cold," Jeff says now, remembering how the wind picked up. How waves crested into white peaks, how gusts buffeted the freshly waxed car and whipped Betty's then-long hair across her face and his, sending them into the back seat where Betty shivered until he got his beach blanket from the trunk and wrapped it tightly around them.

"What?"

"The first time we came here. It got cold."

"Oh," Betty says. "I don't remember."

"How can you not remember? It was the first time we—you know." He recalls laying her back against the gray upholstery, neatly folding his jacket into a pillow for her head. How it should have been clunky and awkward and cramped, but it wasn't. At all. *A good fit,* Betty had said when it was over and they lay there entwined. *We're a good fit.* He twirled the little silver ring around her index finger until it twisted off in his hand. He held it before her. *See this?* She nodded. *I'm going to climb to the top of that distillation column and put it on top. Tomorrow, one of the workers will find it and say to his buddies: Look at this. Some brave fool must sure be in love.* Betty kissed his earlobe as the refinery lights flickered in her eyes.

Tonight Betty says, "This is stupid. The movers are coming tomorrow and I haven't even packed up the kitchen."

Betty is moving back to West Virginia. To White Sulphur Springs to be near her parents and the Greenbrier Resort where she waitressed as a teen. Jeff once asked her if she knew about the resort's secret which had recently been exposed: the super-classified bunker built beneath it for the president and high-ranking officials in case of nuclear attack. *No,* she had said. But she couldn't wait to take the tour, to go through the fat metal door and see the operating room and rows of bunk beds and the incinerator meant to dispose of contaminated bodies. She thinks she dated an FBI agent disguised as a maintenance worker. *His first name was an initial,* she said. *R. That has to mean something.*

In less than a week she'll be gone. Her brother David is flying down to help with the driving. To speed through six states and, Jeff thinks, deliver Betty to Bo, her high school sweetheart though *he's just a good friend,* says Betty. Jeff wonders about that, about Betty's last trip to West Virginia without him. Her father's quadruple bypass and of course she had to be there. Dutiful daughter and all that. She stayed one week, two, extended it to three and a half. When she returned, fat blue envelopes started arriving in the mail. From Bo. When the first letter came Jeff tore it open and read innocuous page after page, but that didn't stop him from flapping it in Betty's face when she came home from work. She said: *He's a whole time zone away, for God's sake. He's going through a divorce and he just needs an ear.* Jeff wonders which other of his wife's body parts Bo needs.

Jeff should be relieved that Betty won't be making the two-day trip by herself. The baby is cutting back molars, and it's scary for a woman alone on the road. Hasn't he told her that five times a day for the past decade? *It's a jungle out there. Be careful.* Besides, Betty no longer has the baseball bat or, Jeff thinks, the courage to use it. He has protected her for so long that whatever muscle she flexed by moving so far from home has atrophied. He does so much for her, so much he's sure she doesn't appreciate, that she'll miss once he's out of her life. It's how he proves his love. Who'll do all that now? Who'll peer in closets and under beds like he did when they came home to a dark house when he was sure he left a light on? Who'll check and recheck and recheck to make sure the deadbolts are locked before going to bed? Who will stand before the refrigerator the first of each month to inspect expiration dates on mayonnaise and ketchup and pickle relish? Who will feel Stephanie's chest in the middle of the night to make sure it's still rising and falling, or call MedLine seven times in a row when she develops a rash? Not Bo. He can't imagine anyone named Bo being that responsible, even if he is a *mining engineer*.

"Jeff," Betty says. "Just take me home. Please."

"Come on. Who knows when you'll be back here. Don't you want to see it one last time before you leave?"

"Not really."

"It'll be fun. Look!" he says, pointing. "There's the sign for Friendswood. We're almost there." He hears Betty's teeth grating so he shuts up and drives, absently counting the dashed white lines which sends him back to his first summer job working for the highway department. Hours and hours of setting out orange cones and barrels in tidy rows to redirect traffic when the roads were repainted, picking them back up when the crew was through. He remembers one afternoon when the heat was so intense it bounced off the concrete in waves. He tied his T-shirt around his forehead and hoisted the barrels onto the back of a flatbed, admiring the crisp dashed white lines, bold double yellows. Then he saw the dead cat, nearly flattened in the middle of the road, double yellow lines painted right over its carcass. He wondered why the crew hadn't scraped it out of the way. It would decompose soon enough leaving a gap in the line. *A gap in the line.* A thousand times since that day, in his mind, he'd peeled up the paint, shoveled out the dead animal, and smoothed the lines back to perfection.

In twenty minutes they reach their turnoff and that sad billboard with the blonde girl's picture, Ashley Wilcox, and the caption: Have you seen me? The first time Jeff saw it, he decided that if his own daughter were kidnapped he would plaster her picture on billboards, too. And flyers, milk cartons. He'd take out television ads, and radio. He would stand in traffic to look in cars. Hire a bloodhound. After Stephanie was born, he constructed a six-foot privacy fence in the backyard, dug the post holes himself, strung the line to make sure it was straight, nailed the boards tightly in place. *Parks aren't safe,* he'd told Betty. *Predators are just waiting to snatch little kids from public parks.* He prefers to stay home and look after his daughter though it's cost him three jobs already. How many mornings had he called in with a lie? *Migraine,* he'd say. Or *bad back.* Though Betty is disgusted with these tactics he is *sure* she understands his apprehension about daycare, about free-floating germs, about under-trained strangers who don't know about Stephanie's allergies to red Kool-Aid and Fig Newtons. He has considered home schooling. He could do it, he thinks. He's taught her so much already: her colors; her letters; the names of tools; that ☠ = poison; don't touch your face until you've thoroughly washed your hands; never *ever* use someone else's bathroom—though this last rule retarded her potty training somewhat.

But tonight, Jeff drives toward the pier, toward the last bit of light hugging the water. The fishermen are in place and he wonders if they could be the same ones as ten years ago. It's possible. Jeff parks and shuts off the engine. Pulls the keys from the ignition. He opens his door and hears the engine tic-tic-tic. He puts one leg outside.

"I'm not getting out," Betty says.

"We're here."

"I don't care. The sooner we get this over with the better."

Jeff looks at his wife, his ex-wife, and can tell by the pucker of her mouth she's not budging. It's the same pucker she wore the day they stopped to pick wild grapes when she was pregnant. Jeff saw her pop one of the grapes in her mouth. He lectured her so thoroughly about bird shit and stray-dog piss and slug slime that not only did she spit out the grape, but she dumped the baseball capful they'd already picked onto the side of the road.

He pulls his foot back inside the car and closes the door. "It's still pretty," he says, trying to recreate the magic, the awe of that first visit. Trying to remind Betty about everything right in their lives. Then maybe she'll call this whole thing off. This whole stupid thing.

"Galveston's busy," he says.

Betty looks across the water at neon restaurant signs and palm trees strung with white twinkling lights.

"You want a jaw breaker?"

Betty laughs and Jeff is relieved that he's finally hit upon a pleasant bit of their history. They used go to Galveston on Saturdays and walk The Strand, the historic town center, stop in that candy store that sold jaw breakers the size of nectarines. Betty would work on one side of it the entire ride home until her tongue bled. Ooing and ahhing at the striated layers of color her labor revealed. *Like the earth's core*, she once said. Then she'd wrap it up and put it in the vegetable bin in the refrigerator, along with the other half-sucked remnants of past trips—the only perishable Jeff didn't have the heart to throw out. Tomorrow, if he can't change her mind, she'll pull open that drawer and spill dozens and dozens of lop-sided jaw breakers into the trash. They will clunk together at the bottom like golf balls.

Betty rests the swan on the floor and digs through her purse. "Here," she says, pulling out a Ziploc bag. "I might as well give this to you now."

"What is it?" Jeff says, not lifting his hand, not wanting to take whatever guilt offering or booby prize is inside.

"Just, here," she says, opening it up, pulling out Stephanie's hospital picture. Jeff clicks on the dome light and takes it, looks at his daughter's purple face, the dumb pink bow taped to her head, little fists balled up. He wonders if this is the only photo he will get, though there are six albums worth of Polaroids he snapped weekly and arranged and labeled with Sharpie permanent ink.

"And this," Betty says, handing him the trilobite they found at Enchanted Rock. Jeff takes the bag and pulls out the silver bolo tie Betty bought him at the rodeo in the Astrodome. There's a coin tucked into a cardboard and cellophane holder. The letters JAG and the year 1818 are stamped on one side, a tiny lone star on the other.

"You're giving me this?"

"They're your initials," she says, referring to the reason they paid four dollars for it at a roadside flea market. Only later did they take it to a coin dealer and find out that it was early Texas money: a New Spain Jola, a half real, coined by Jose Antonio de la Garza. Worth three-thousand bucks.

"I figured you could sell it," she says.

Don't do me any favors, he wants to say. "I'm not going to sell it."

"Don't be an idiot, Jeff. I know you could use the money."

Jeff zips the coin, the photo, the trilobite, the bolo tie back into the baggy and tucks it inside his jacket pocket. "Maybe I'll give it to Stephanie."

Betty let's out a little sigh. "Whatever," she says. "But wait till she's older so she doesn't choke on it."

Jeff feels like he's the one choking. *When she's older*, he thinks, fingers thumping on the seat beside him as he imagines his daughter's first whole sentences edged not with his lilting Texas drawl, but with that tinny backward twang he once found so endearing. Still does, really. He's going to miss playing Santa, and the piano lessons they always talked about. Who will make sure she's immunized, pull her baby teeth, teach her the names of birds? Who will show her how to look right-left-right-left-right-left before crossing the street? To yell FIRE! when strangers approach. To not accept unwrapped Halloween candy.

"Do you have to take her so far?" he says, fingers drumming wildly.

Betty presses her hand over his to stop the noise. "We've been through this."

Jeff pulls his hand out from under hers. They have been through this, time after time: Betty's financial stability, her family network, her maternal rights. Her ridiculous mislabeling of his orderliness, of his parental concern. *Obsession*, she called it. *Neurosis.*

"Please just take me home," Betty says.

Jeff nods, turns off the dome light, and starts the car. Before pulling out he looks over at Texas City. A blue flame billows from a venting column, yellow tip licking the sky.

Back on I-45 Jeff stays in the left lane doing below the speed limit.

"I think I've got a job lined up back home," Betty says.

"What?"

"Just a receptionist at the Greenbrier, but it's a start. Talk about coming full circle."

Jeff squints in the rearview, trying desperately to catch a glimpse of the refineries. "Who's going to look after Stephanie?"

"Mom and Dad."

He feels a real migraine coming. "They barely look after themselves."

"They take care of David's kids just fine."

Jeff bites his tongue, picturing Stephanie skipping around Betty's parents' house. Tripping on their slippery area rugs. Bumping her head on their brick fireplace. Sticking her curious fingers into nonchildproofed electrical sockets while her seventy-five-year-old grand-parents chase after David's two wild boys. He doesn't even want to imagine what the boys will do to torment, to torture her.

"Can't she just stay here with me?" Jeff whispers.

"You're living in someone's spare bedroom, Jeff. You don't have a job."

"I'll get one. I'll keep one, for her."

"And who'll watch her while *you're* at work?"

Pressure builds behind Jeff's left eye. "Betty," he whispers, "she's the only thing I ever really did right."

Betty looks at him, at his lower jaw sagging. "I'm sorry," she says. "But it's not going to happen."

An eighteen-wheeler roars through Jeff's brain and he floors the gas pedal to outrun it, speedometer edging past 50-60-70-80.

"Jeff," Betty says, voice low and flat. "Slow down."

He doesn't listen, practically stands on the gas as the startled engine trembles and whines.

Betty grips the dashboard as they pass car after car on the right, left, weaving dangerously close to their bumpers. A Toyota honks and flashes its lights.

"Stop it!" Betty yells.

Jeff doesn't stop and the needle is out of numbers but he wants to go faster, get the hell home where Stephanie sleeps in her sturdy bed with fire-retardant mattresses and sheets and pajamas, smoke alarms and carbon monoxide detectors surrounding her like a force field.

Suddenly Jeff slams on the brakes. The car fishtails and swerves, tires screeching as he veers off the road.

When the car settles Betty glares over. "You trying to kill us?" she says, face ashen, looking as if she believes, at this moment, he is capable of such a thing.

"I saw a dog," he says, jamming the car in park. He gets out without closing the door.

"Come back here!" Betty calls over the incessant ding-ding-ding, the car's complaint that the keys are still in the ignition.

Vehicles he so recklessly passed just minutes before pass him now. Some drivers honk, shake their fists. One guy gives him the finger. Jeff doesn't care. He starts walking, following his skid marks, gravel crunching under his boots. He hears a hum overhead and looks up at power lines strung from electrical towers spaced out like dominoes across the scrubby field to his left, leading back to Texas City. "Here, pooch!" he calls, looking for the mutt he's sure he saw trotting in the middle of the road.

"Jeff!" Betty calls, but he keeps walking, squinting, scouring the road for the animal and there it is. A tangle of dingy fur sauntering between the north and southbound lanes, eyes glinting from the cars' headlights whipping by on both sides.

Jeff squats across from it on the berm, and when the road is clear he holds out a hand. "Come here, pup," he calls, voice warm and inviting. The dog stops, lowers her head, but her tail sways as Jeff makes kissy sounds. The dog looks at Jeff, then back up the highway, considering.

"I've got food!" Jeff yells, standing, slowly walking backward to the car. The dog walks, too, still in the center of the road. "You hungry?" Jeff calls over. "Wait'll you see what I got." When Jeff nears the car Betty rattles the keys at him. "I need to get home!"

"Give me your leftovers."

"What?"

"Your leftovers. I can lure her over."

"No! I don't want a stinky dog in here."

Normally Jeff wouldn't either, but something about this dog, this night, makes him forget about ringworm and flea infestation and he reaches in and snatches the swan by Betty's feet.

"You ass!" she says, as he unfolds the foil, exposing tender bits of rare steak, lobster, a dinner roll. He kneels, gravel jabbing his knees, and sets the bait down. The dog stops and faces Jeff, tongue lolling, but she won't cross.

When the road is clear Jeff says: "Here!" and hurls a bit of meat at her. The dog hears where it hits and sniffs in frantic circles until she finds it and gobbles it down. She looks over, licking her chops.

He tosses another hunk of meat which she gulps without chewing and looks at him expectantly. "Oh no," Jeff says. "You have to come get it." He steps away from the foil to give her a wide berth. She eyes the food and takes a step toward it, but stops.

"It's all right," Jeff says. "Come on."

She takes another step into the road but an RV zooms dangerously close, ruffling her fur, coating Jeff in a gritty spray.

"Jeff, get in the car!" Betty yells.

Jeff doesn't listen. He squats down by the car's rear tire to appear less imposing, marveling at the dog's street smarts as she watches and waits for cars to pass, then darts across the road and pounces on the food. As she snarfs it down, Jeff sees her sagging teats. "She's just had pups!" he says.

"Then leave her be!" Betty says. "She's probably heading back to them right now."

"No. She's lost," he says with such certainty he almost believes it. "She'll get hit if we don't help her."

"She's fine!" Betty says. "Get in this car!"

Jeff takes one step toward the dog, then another, another. He knows that if he can just wrap his arms tightly around her he can drag her into the car where it's safe. The dog frantically licks the foil, desperate for every grease dripping, every bread crumb. She's too engrossed, Jeff thinks, to notice, to care that he's almost upon her, arms wide, ready to encircle, but the second he reaches forward she jerks her head around and bites his opened hand.

"Son of a bitch!" he yowls, yanking his hand back while the dog snatches the foil and runs into the field.

"What!" Betty calls. "What happened?"

"She bit me," Jeff says, shaking his hand as if that'll dispel the pain. Betty slides over the bench seat and gets out. "Let me see."

"It's all right," he says, pressing the skin to see if blood beads form. "Did it break the skin?"

"No," Jeff says, pulling out his shirt tail to blot up dog slobber, resisting the urge to check the glove box for a Sani-Wipe.

"Well thank heavens for that."

"I've got to get her," he says, looking out across the field where the dog has stopped to work on the foil.

"She'll bite you again. She may have rabies."

"She doesn't have rabies," Jeff says, heading into scrub brush that tugs at his pants.

"How do you know?" Betty calls. She steps toward him but her high heels wobble and tip in the dirt. "Get back here!" she screams.

Jeff pushes his legs through patches of knee-high bramble, keeping sight of the dog who keeps one eye on him.

"It's okay!" he calls to her, offering comfort and assurance as he fiercely tries to save her life. But as soon as he's within twenty feet she abandons the foil and bolts deeper into the field, zigzagging under power lines, the hum so loud Jeff feels his bones vibrating. He starts chasing her, leaping over mesquite and sage, ducking under electrical towers. He hears a car horn screaming and looks back at Betty, leaning in the car, frantically pounding the horn. "I swear to God I'll leave you here if you don't come back right now!"

When he turns back around he can't find the dog. He stops and squints to his right, his left, looking for movement, for rustling weeds, but there's nothing. If he could just see over the brush—and before the thought registers he heads for the next electrical tower which looks so much like a mini oil derrick except for three pairs of outstretched metallic arms on top gripping the thick wires. He grabs the framework and hauls himself up though it's difficult climbing since much of the grid work is welded in at angles, his boots sliding down. He hoists himself higher and higher, muscles straining, sweat already dripping, the buzz growing louder in his ears, his brain, and the frantic honk-honk-honk as his wife pounds the horn, her muffled shouts.

Halfway up he pauses on a level bar and looks over the field, mostly in shadows, and surveys the land around him. Nothing. A slight breeze chills the damp streaks on his face and he cranes his head southeast to look at Texas City, lights clearly visible along the horizon. He wonders if some man stands in steel-toed boots on a venting column or cat cracker right now, looking in his direction, wondering about him, too. He looks back at the car, at Betty waving her arms. And though he knows she is angry, he also hopes she remembers and is impressed by his mettle, by the lengths he'd go through to save a poor stray though he doubts he'll ever find the dog now. But Betty doesn't know that, and the thought sends him higher, toward those metallic arms opened wide to receive him.

As he climbs, he feels Betty's eyes on him and he knows this is the moment he so desperately needs. He reaches the next level cross beam and plants his boots firmly on it, though it cuts into his soles. When he feels stable, steady, he begins to release his hand grip. He will show Betty something about courage. He releases his fingers and pulls his hands slowly, slowly away from the bar, his feet teetering slightly for balance as he raises his arms high above his head to show her, to remind her, so that when he comes down she will run to him, wrap her arms tightly around him, gloriously impressed and relieved.

The air horn blast startles him and his feet tip back and forth, arms flail just a bit before Jeff grabs hold of the bar and squeezes tight. He inhales twice before looking down at Betty, talking to a burly trucker who has pulled his rig behind the Monte Carlo. She points up at Jeff and wipes at something under her eyes. The trucker heads into the field and Betty crosses her arms over her chest and looks at him. Even from this distance Jeff can read her weary face, a face grown tired from night after night of sitting on the edge of Stephanie's bed—as he has seen her do so many times—to explain that it's all right to sit in the grass, that worms are *good*, that the boogie man will *not* get in the back door if we don't check it five times; that her teeth won't fall out if she doesn't use a new toothbrush every week even if that's what Daddy says.

Jeff looks at his hands gripping the steel, how dirty they must be, covered in industrial fallout and diesel spray. He has an overwhelming urge to climb down and scrub his hands with the Lifebuoy soap he keeps stockpiled, and that special soft-wire brush for under his nails, the bristles now flattened by his rough usage. Just last week he watched Stephanie drag her plastic step stool to the sink, pull down the Lifebuoy and hold it under a stream of cool water just as she watched her father do a hundred, a thousand times. She grabbed the brush and tried to drag it across her nails, clumsily mimicking her father's bold strokes, his counting: one-humma-humma, two-humma-humma, three-humma-humma. He thought it was cute until she screamed and jumped off her stool, tender fingertips slightly bleeding, but bleeding nonetheless.

He squeezes his eyes shut when the full realization hits him, of what he has done, is doing, to his daughter. For a moment he can see into a future where she's too embarrassed to have sleepovers because her dad will label the guest's drinking glass or pillowcase. Or worse, she won't invite them at all for fear that they will contaminate her room. It's a future where she is afraid of public restrooms and restaurant silverware and trying on clothes at department stores because you don't know who tried them on last.

When he opens his eyes he peers into the night sky at blinking stars. The disk of the moon. A jet plane soars overhead and he pictures the cabin filled with sleepy passengers flipping through flight magazines or watching second-rate films, their thoughts back on earth with the families they are leaving behind, or speeding toward— families that long for the missing member's return.

Jeff looks back at the ground, at Betty, who no longer looks at him. He follows her gaze which zooms past coastal plains, swampland, and finally into the foothills of the Alleghenies, back to West Virginia, White Sulphur Springs, to Bo, a man who will likely have no problem letting Stephanie make mud pies, or drink out of water fountains, or go to public pools.

A fist clenches in Jeff's chest and he knows that Betty is right to move on, to move away, with their daughter.

Still squinting into the northeastern sky, Jeff conjures a vision of the Greenbrier Resort: crisp white facade, sturdy rows of columns, circular gardens of red and white tulips. But underneath. Underneath. And for a moment the fist in his chest releases at the thought of his daughter tucked deep inside that secret bunker with the thick metal door that will protect her, will keep her safe, now that he can't.

"Come on down, buddy," a voice calls. Jeff looks below at the trucker standing at the base of the tower, one foot propped on a beam, ready to ascend. He would do it, Jeff thinks. Come and fetch some poor lunatic for the frantic damsel on the side of the road.

"I'm coming," Jeff answers, but before taking a step he tugs that Ziploc from his jacket and palpates the goods inside. Not much to show for the last ten years of his life—except for Stephanie, of course. He takes out her picture and runs his thumb over it in the moon's glow before sliding it in his back pocket. The Ziploc, though, he wedges securely in the crook where two metal bars meet. Only then does he descend, slowly, one careful foot after another, but his mind already races into the future, fastening on the image of a maintenance worker coming to inspect the tower, maybe in a month, a year, two years. Jeff imagines the look on the lineman's face when he finds the bag. He will wonder about the trilobite, the bolo tie, the New Spain Jola. Maybe he will discover the coin's value. Or maybe it'll sit in the back of his junk drawer for the next fifty years. But mostly, Jeff thinks, he will wonder about the kind of man who would leave such treasure behind.

Still Life with Plums

The jet shoots like a missile through the westward sky. Natalie bends toward the sun outside the portal, the cadmium ball searing negative images of itself onto her eyelids when she closes them. But she can't keep them shut for long with that frigid itch in her veins. Leaving her convalescing mother in James's hands. She doesn't know who to feel sorrier for. Well James, of course, with her mother's incessant ramblings.

Natalie shuffles her feet, nudging the leather satchel in the footwell stuffed with scraps of her new novel, the one she has been chiseling at for over twenty years. She lugs it with her everywhere—doctors' appointments, the vets—like a bagful of sins. She pulls a book from her purse about the bonobo chimps, research for the novel—changing metaphors yet again—captivated by photos of verdant central African jungles. Ironic, Natalie thinks, given her destination: the Sonoran Desert.

The trip is a gift from Natalie's truest friend, Beth, a former college classmate. *Two workshops and a few meetings with awe-struck students,* Beth cajoled. *And we'll write you an outrageous check.*

Natalie had nearly turned Beth down. *I don't know,* she mewled into the phone. *This is getting ridiculous. How can I call myself a writer if I don't even write?*

Quit being so fucking precious, Beth stabbed. *Get your ass on the plane. When you get here we'll shoot tequila and run naked through the desert.*

Natalie envisioned the desert: skittering lizards, parched heat, miles and miles of sand. A few arid days to thaw out her bones after being snowed in for the winter in the Eastern Panhandle, the last few grueling weeks of it with her broken-hipped mother. The double lure was time away from James. Away from the same old tension they'd been writhing in for years: Natalie's discontent that she couldn't articulate because words failed her there, too. "Is it me?" James would prod. *No.* "Is it another man?" *No.* "Are you worried about Nathan?" their son in Iraq. *Of course, but it's more than that.* "Then what the hell is it?" *I don't know.*

As added incentive, at that very moment Natalie's mother crowed from the guestroom down the hall: *Natalie! Get the bedpan. Quick!*

Yes, Natalie told Beth. *God yes, I'll come.*

Circling overhead, Arizona is both greener and beiger than Natalie expected, a Cezanne quilt flapped across the desert floor and up over the Tucson Mountains. Not like the footage of barren sand she views nightly on CNN. No desert life there, at least not that she can spy from so very far away. She wonders what Nathan is doing this very minute. What time it is for him since he is eight hours ahead of West Virginia. Ten hours ahead of Tucson. *Sleeping*, she thinks, she hopes, and suddenly she can feel the newborn weight of him in her arms, the way she rocked and cooed and never wanted to lay him down. Ever.

The baggage carousel labors under its shifting, man-handled load. Natalie skims the mostly-black suitcases and spots her yellow one—a toucan in the rain forest. She hoists it down and starts toward Ground Transportation when she hears the familiar thwap-thwap of flip-flops against tile. It's Beth, accompanied by her annoying scuffing habit, sporting a new spiked, bleached hairdo. Natalie is always dismayed by the change in this once-meek girl who barely raised her hand in class and tried to fold herself inside a three-foot curtain of auburn hair. It's a stunning role reversal since Beth pursued the Ph.D., Natalie's long-ago plan that would support her writing habit, a path she ultimately didn't need or take, a nagging insecurity about her literary credentials regardless of her laurels. And with each year that she does not finish her *long-awaited second book* she finds herself lunging for her own imaginary hair curtain to hide behind.

Beth opens welcoming arms as she approaches. "Oprah?" she shouts still from several feet away, the words echoing off distant walls. "You're a fucking Oprah classic pick now?"

Natalie's head flops forward. "I confess."

"Greedy bitch," Beth adds, gripping Natalie in her sturdy arms. "You lucky, greedy bitch."

Natalie doesn't feel lucky though she knows she should. Still so much money coming in from her first novel, *Mixed Metaphors*, written in a six-month frenzy as an undergrad when she was pregnant and all she could stomach was tomato soup and Cheetos. How her little book catapulted skyward until she was absurdly lauded The Voice of Her Age. VoHA, Beth jabs. Frequently. *The Divine Ms. VoHA.*

In the parking lot, Natalie draws hot air into her lungs, imagines her blood thickening as she peels off her jacket, her sweater, marveling that just hours before she was shivering on an icy tarmac miles to the east. As Beth drives away from the airport she chatters wildly—another verbose woman—about her recent move to Arizona, her new teaching post to escape her old life. *Such a brave leap,* Natalie thinks as they aim for distant mountains, the folds and peaks looking like loads of rumpled towels dumped still warm from the dryer. Natalie relaxes into the gentle ascension, the unexpected dashes of yellow and magenta against the burnt earth, the bramble and brush, the saguaro hailing her like old friends. Or perhaps offering a thorny warning: *Turn back!*

After several minutes she realizes that Beth has stopped talking. "I loved *The Temple of Tikal,*" Natalie confesses about Beth's latest book, the sixth in a series of international murder mysteries.

"If only the snotty-literati would take notice," Beth says, "but then it's no *Mixed Metaphors,*" their standing joke.

"Well, what is?" Natalie says, wishing the snotty-literati could forget about her, that cluster of old white men who have rented a smoky room in the dark part of her brain where they drink scotch and sharpen their knives. They all look and sound exactly like George Plimpton, though occasionally her dead father pulls up a chair, too.

A jackrabbit skitters across the road and Beth doesn't even slow down.

"Seriously," Natalie says. "You're disgustingly prolific."

"I just plant my ass in the chair two hours a day," Beth says. "It's not magic."

Isn't it magic? Natalie wants to ask, but she knows better. Beth is not a romantic, nor has she apparently rented out any critical parts of her brain.

Beth pauses at a stop light and looks over at Natalie.

Don't ask. Don't ask. Don't ask, Natalie's well-practiced incantation when she's afraid someone's going to probe about her new book.

"Don't worry. I was just going to ask how James likes country living."

"We're an hour from D.C. It's not exactly remote."

"Still, why did you buy a five-bedroom farmhouse now? And what in the world do you need twenty acres for?"

Natalie doesn't know the answer to that. She really does not. "I had to do something with all that Oprah money."

Beth throws her head back and guffaws. "Well at least you can put some distance between yourself and your mother."

Natalie presses her chin to her chest. "I wish," she says, but even now she can hear her mother's nasally voice that penetrates every room, every closet, the listing barn out back, the rickety fort built in the mulberry tree at the farthest corner of the property. She wonders if her mother magically packed her voice in Natalie's satchel so it would assail her even here: *Natalie, did I tell you about the time* . . . .

It is exactly the kind of resort Natalie expected: a cluster of flat-topped adobe structures in earthen tones, all looking as if they had been carved out of desert rock by indigenous people. Natalie makes a note to find out exactly which tribe that might have been. Another possible metaphor: a whole clan scattered like sand, leaving only the remnants of past villages now just calcified bones being overrun by camera-wielding ants. Could the original builders ever have imagined such a thing when they chiseled doorways and rooms out of solid rock? Piled stone upon stone. Lashed together precious timber. Hewed out troughs for their animals. A sudden fantasy rumble of stampeding bison, an archaic echo still whirling across the earth for hundreds, maybe thousands of years.

Natalie is assigned half of a duplex bungalow across the gravel road from the lodge. Beth lugs in the suitcase and plops it on the bed, the coiled springs complaining. On the bedside table sits a cellophane-wrapped gift basket filled with cans of tomato soup and Cheetos.

"Just trying to jumpstart the juices," Beth says.

Natalie laughs, but that particular ritual lost its power years ago. And she has tried.

"Can't help you with the knocked-up part, but I made sure there are a few cute boys in your workshop."

Natalie thumps her belly. "No uterus, remember?"

"Uterus, schmuterous."

After Beth leaves, Natalie sinks into an overstuffed chair by the window, the sun basting her with heat. She opens her satchel and bypasses her novel and her mother's voice to pull out the workshop manuscripts. Eight short stories that she has already read and scribbled on. All skillfully written. Lots of terse man-stories chock with gratuitous violence and cigarettes. Plenty of self-absorbed, struggling-writer vignettes that make Natalie wince. There is one, however, that she has read three times, pencil at the ready, without etching a single mark. She riffles the bundle and finds it: "The Lemons are Crying" by Hannah Pasqual, though there isn't a lemon in it and nobody cries. It is exactly like so many stories Natalie has been reading lately by all those up-and-coming writers. Gorgeous words, sentences, whole paragraphs packed with lush metaphors ripe with meanings Natalie can't quite piece together, but how she desperately wants to. Sentient animals with exquisite vocabularies. Houses that walk. Trees that take baths and benevolent lawns. It's not Magical Realism exactly. Beyond Fabulist by far. She keeps looking for the story. *Where's the story?* she often whispers as she reads, afraid she ineptly missed it. Even now, in her chair, Natalie's heart hammers in the same way it did when she tried to chip through *Ulysses* and finally gave up after page sixty-five, a secret failure, especially for a writer who is The Voice of Her Age. Because it is as if these wordsmiths have tapped a rich stratum deep inside the earth that Natalie has been unable to mine for such a very long time, if ever at all.

A fluke, one critic wrote years ago about *Mixed Metaphors. One hit wonder,* she has read more and more frequently. (Oh, but what a hit, Beth has often consoled.) *Fluke.* Natalie tumbles the word around in her mouth. Feels the weight of it on her tongue and then etched on the roof of her mouth like a cave drawing, an image that erupted after she researched the Paleolithic drawings of Lascaux Caves, such primal imagery, ripe for double meaning: horse, bison, fluke. She runs her tongue over the five letters forming sans-serif legs and a tail, arched neck, a raised head bleating the very word.

Natalie arrives late to eat dinner in the lodge with the rest of the faculty: two more aging fiction writers and three poets all with yard-long CVs and stacks of published books. They greet her through clenched teeth as they vigorously carve up their meat, steel cutlery click-clacking. For two solid hours they bemoan academia, such little time to write, how lucky Natalie is (words coated with thorns), the grief they suffer from their high-brow colleagues who disrespect their *creative* pursuits, an odd conundrum. But these writers have scholarly leanings as well: all that lit crit and theory, post-post this, meta-that, hyper-whatever that Natalie grew bored with years ago, preferring the much more fascinating dissection of simple people navigating through difficult lives. Still, all this pedantic lexicon makes her pleat and unpleat her napkin in her lap, a hundred done and un-done paper birds, until the ball-peen thrumming on her solar plexus is too much and she excuses herself to use the restroom.

She passes two women reconnecting at the salad bar offering hugs and kisses and "Haven't seen you since Yaddo! Or was it Breadloaf?" Such a weird subculture, Natalie thinks. A carnival circuit for writers and she wonders what sideshow freak that makes her: tattooed lady; one hit wonder; wordless woman.

That night in bed Natalie learns that bonobo and Homo sapiens DNA is 98% identical. Unlike the common chimpanzee, the bonobos' facial features vary slightly, like humans, so they can tell each other apart. Natalie brushes her fingers over her face, feels the sharp bend in her nose, the divot in her chin, the zygomatic arch of bone that runs from her temple to her cheek. She wonders if James would be able to identify her solely by touch in a darkened cave. She could certainly identify him, and Nathan. Natalie looks at her right hand, no coarse throwback hairs, though the bulging knuckles are regrettable, the stubby fingernails she passed along to her son. But not to her daughter, her second and surprisingly last child, fully-formed, stillborn, who had James's lovely almond-shaped nails.

Natalie slides her thumb over the callus on her middle finger where a stand-worth of cedar pencils have rested over the years—because she still writes in longhand—hoping the ritual that had worked so well that one time will once again prove fruitful, even if tomato soup and Cheetos no longer do.

At home, every night, she grips a pencil firmly for hours and hours, etching words and phrases until she depresses a shallow trench in the now-thickened flesh. She wants to tell Beth that. *I do sit my ass in the chair!* One day the trench will set for good, Natalie thinks, wondering if it will be worth it, all those words. But to be honest, she has scrawled more doodles than prose over the years. Carousels and biplanes when Nathan was small. Gibberish stories they penned together about helium-filled tadpoles and stackable turtles. Clouds that play ping-pong. Hiccupping lakes. She has years and years of elaborate mazes and spirals. M.C. Escher stairways and interlocking geese. But Nathan outgrew all that, leaving Natalie alone in her office with spiral notebooks of too bright paper. Hours of writing the same words over and over until they lost all meaning: livelylivelylivelylivelylivelywiltwiltwiltwiltwilt. She has considered the possibility that she has spent her lifetime allotment of words.

Natalie flosses and brushes her teeth to unclog the Cheetos goo stuck in her gums—because even if they have lost their charm she still loves the taste. She washes her face with a bar of gritty natural soap beside the sink that she had to unwrap like a precious gift, reminding her of that unearthed dead woman on the History Channel whose flesh had turned into soap. She imagines the grit and speckles in her herbal bar are bone chips and fingernails. Surprisingly, she is not grossed out. Afterwards her skin feels tight so she rustles through her cosmetic bag for the fancy face cream James's younger sister Joyce gave her for Christmas for maturing skin. *You trying to tell me something?* Natalie asked. The better gift was the jewelry box Joyce's three girls, ten-year-old fertility-drug triplets, constructed out of tongue depressors, alphabet macaroni, and gummi bears.

Natalie slides off her wedding ring to keep the thick cream from gunking up the setting. It's an emerald-cut diamond James picked out himself while still in engineering school and paid too much for. The intricate platinum setting, such detailed work. She holds the ring to the light and imagines a decrepit jeweler bent over his table, squinting through his loupe with rheumy eyes so he can better craft her particular ring. And then she remembers that documentary she watched on conflict diamonds in West Africa, another transient metaphor until that movie with Leonardo DiCaprio brought it to global attention and put the skids on it for her. Nothing fresh about that. But as she watched the film she twisted her diamond around and around her finger wondering if it was mined with enforced labor. If James traded his hard-earned cab driver's salary for guns, or machetes, or whatever weapons wielded to exert power.

A sudden image of Nathan in his desert fatigues. That picture he sent of himself and his two buddies, green bullet-proof vests strapped around their torsos, beige helmets shading most of their faces, black rifles or machine guns (Natalie doesn't know the difference, nor does she want to know) looped over their shoulders, held in their hands as tenderly as if they were alive. Ribbons of ammo spilling out like entrails.

A peal of laughter from the lodge across the road brings such relief that Natalie clatters the ring on the counter and lunges across the room, thinly parts the curtain to peer out. Under the lodge's yellow porch lights she spies a cluster of youthful conferees settling into a row of Adirondack chairs. One young man hoists himself onto the porch railing and stretches his arms overhead to grip the rafters. When he has a firm hold he lets his legs swing free so he can sway back and forth, back and forth, his troop mates whooping and chattering.

Hours later the occupants of the other half of Natalie's duplex struggle to open their door. A man and woman giggling, stumbling inside, blurting out words like "Shit" and "Ow" and "Hurry the fuck up." Natalie pulls her pillow over her head but it won't drown out the sound of their urgent coupling, the mattress creaking, the headboard battering the wall. A cliché of all the bad sex scenes she has watched in B movies and it's over so quickly Natalie is embarrassed for them. She hears their TV click on, a man-powered movie with car chases and explosions, helicopter blades whop-whop-whopping. She knows there will be no sleeping now.

The next morning, eyes gritty, Natalie arrives five minutes late to her first workshop, banana and canned apple juice in hand, a calculated tardiness since she hates waiting, hates the discomfort, the throat-clearing as the class assembles and tries to figure out how to behave around her.

She pauses outside the open door to take a swish of juice to loosen her tongue and catches snippets of hushed dialogue. "I heard this is her last conference," someone says. "After this she's going to hole up like Salinger. Is he even still alive?" "I don't know, but I heard they're paying her ten-thousand bucks for three days." "I heard she and Beth were lovers back in college." Natalie chokes on her juice, burning the back of her throat. She coughs and gasps, shutting up everyone in the room.

Natalie steps into the abyss as all those eyes peer at her, expecting authority she tries her best to pull off since, according to their bios, many of these writers are far more educated than she. She scans their faces, mostly young, Nathan's age, but some middle-aged and older all looking back at her.

The conference table is horseshoe-shaped and the one spare chair is dead center at the top of the U or the bottom. Natalie aims for it, spotting several copies of *Mixed Metaphors* among the students' conference folders. Hardback and soft. She's delighted to see one with the original dust jacket, tattered and yellowed. She always loved that particular cover—a Kandinsky painting which exactly expressed her mood at the time. It was that first edition she inscribed for her father: *Thanks for the push.* Some of the students' books are the most recent edition, the cover forgettable except for the blue Oprah seal. Natalie hopes she brought her good book-signing gel pen. *With warm regards . . . . With fond memories of our meeting . . . . With the hopes of one day reading your book . . . .*

"Good morning," Natalie says.

A whir of jumbled pleasantries that sounds like a flock of alighting sparrows.

"I want to begin by asking each of you to tell me your name and why you began writing."

She starts every workshop with this banal icebreaker because there's always plenty of material even if she's heard most of the stories: *I've always written; I love to read; it's an innate need; I can't not do it; it's my only voice; it's like breathing.*

She's usually more attentive, but as they work around the room, Natalie wonders how she would answer that question today: *Because my father put all his eggs in one basket.* She can hear Beth add, *But what a basket.*

"My name is Hannah Pasqual."

The voice plucks Natalie from her misery. It belongs to a girl, a simple, average-looking girl wearing jeans and a T-shirt. Not dressed in all black. No multiple piercings or funky hairstyle. Neither is she too skinny nor in need of a shower—the greasy-haired, pallid look popular among so many East coast writers these days.

"Because words have colors," she nearly whispers, eyes on her hands. "When I write it's like painting."

One of the boys, Brad, says, "At MacDowell you said words have smells and writing is like cooking."

"It's my simile; I can say what I want," she says, still whispering, her face crimson.

No truer words, Natalie thinks, similar to the ones her father intoned when he not-so-gently steered her toward writing. *Just write for yourself,* a lie, since he ultimately wanted her to write down his stories which all began the same way. *Back in Pittsburgh, when I was a boy.* Her mother's inevitable interruption: *Don't forget to tell her about*—His silencing rant: *Shut up, woman. Shut up, shut up, shut up!* Which she did, finally, for thirty solid years. Until the day her husband died when her lips unsealed and the phone calls started: *Natalie, did I tell you, back in Pittsburgh, when I was a girl*—Natalie's impolite lies: *Sorry Mom. Gotta go write. Big deadline, you know.* She can't get away that easily now.

The first workshop goes smoothly enough. They critique four manuscripts. It's a gabby bunch, all that posturing and showing off what they learned at Iowa or Columbia. They all write so beautifully: beautiful words, beautiful sentences, beautiful paragraphs. Whole pages jam-packed with so much loveliness that Natalie unexpectedly blurts: "Yes, but sometimes the characters just have to come into the room and sit down."

They all stare at her, dumbly, for perhaps half a second before they resume their frenzied ramblings. Except for Hannah Pasqual, who has spent the entire class scribbling in her spiral notebook. She doesn't utter a peep and Natalie tries to imagine what fantasy she is penning:

The stucco walls can't survive all that gabbling. So much drywall and wood meant only to withstand the southwestern heat, the sandstorms, but they are no match for the barrage of words. The inane utterings of all those mouths mimicking other writers' voices: Faulkner, O'Connor, Carver, McCarthy. Here's how to write a blue story. Now write a red one. Countless beautiful words that amount to nothing. But the assault of language is relentless; the liquid syllables a steady stream that sloughs off the flat avocado paint. Worms a wet toehold in the plasterboard until the gritty compound breaks down. Now a puncture in the outer wall, too, where the words pour through, funneling out into the desert which can't drink them in fast enough. A deluge of words catching on shrubs and sagebrush, tangled up in cacti. The words fumbling and bumbling into tumbleweeds roiling eastward, sprouting sanserif legs and heads until it's a stampede of words, their gaping mouths bleating a primal cry: fluke!

Most of the students find little value in the last submission of the day though Natalie thinks it's quite rich. A straightforward story (*a story at last*) written by Peggy, a fifty-something court reporter. Natalie watches Peggy's placid face as the students poke and prod. She could not care less, it seems. Natalie knows she shouldn't assume but she wonders if the woman in the story boiling mason jars is Peggy. There is such longing in each scene, such emptiness. Empty rooms. Empty jars. Empty apron pocket though the woman knows she put her To-Do list in it that very morning. How will she know what to do?

"Nothing happens," Brad says. "It's just an old lady bumbling around in her house."

"What do you mean nothing happens?" It's Hannah Pasqual.

"I mean nothing happens. She makes breakfast. Checks the empty mailbox. Cans fruit. Maybe if there were a few more characters."

"She owns a peach orchard," Hannah says. "She's surrounded by peach trees dripping with life."

"All she does is look at them through the window and can plums. And she hates plums."

"Exactly!" Hannah says. "That's exactly the point."

Peggy's eyes glisten like agates.

That afternoon Natalie lopes across the gravel road to her bungalow and closes the rubber-backed curtains to seal out the stark light. She digs her cell phone from her purse and punches in the digits that will connect her to home.

James picks up on the third ring. "Hello?"

"Hey," she says, conjuring exuberance to masquerade her guilt. "How's it going?"

"Great. It's going great," he says. Natalie wonders if he's conjuring his own exuberance.

"How's Mom?"

"Listen for yourself," James says, holding the phone toward Natalie's mother who chatters frantically in the distance.

"God," Natalie says, guilt doubled. "Why don't you slip a Xanax in her Jell-O?"

"It's fine," James says.

"Times like these I wish I had a sibling to pawn her off on," Natalie says, because she, too, was sadly and surprisingly an only child.

"Honestly, it's fine," James says. "Mixed in with all the gibberish are some interesting stories."

"Really?" Natalie says, unexpectedly relieved since she thought she might have stoppered her mother up for good during their last conversation when Natalie was preparing for this trip: scribbling down important phone numbers, arranging for the day nurse, searching for the Dramamine, lining up her mother's pills, trying to dig her good shoes from the high shelf in the closet with her mother droning on and on like a swarm of wasps until Natalie's temples throbbed and she finally and uncharacteristically seethed: *Shut up, woman! Shut up, shut up, shut up!* Which her mother did, leaving Natalie to skulk away in shame. Apparently her mother has more fortitude than she did thirty years ago, a realization that makes Natalie proud.

Natalie turns off her phone, collapses onto her bed, and waits for the falling sensation that means sleep is coming. She sees plums in her mind. Whole bins of stacked purple-blue plums, so plump she wants to reach her hand in and pull one out so they will tumble and spill with soft thuds at her feet. But the plums turn into lemons and saliva gushes from under her tongue at the memory of tartness. The lemons disappear when Natalie hears the shower being turned on next door, the resounding thud, not of plums, but bare feet on fiberglass, a bar of falling soap (speckled with fingernails and bone, no doubt). A man starts humming *Ode to Joy* quite beautifully. The whir of metal loops sliding against the rod as the shower curtain is whipped aside. "Surprise!" It's the girl.

"Come here," the man orders. More feet pummeling fiberglass, then elbows banging the walls, guttural moans. Squeals and peals of ecstasy.

"I give up," Natalie says, sitting up to turn on the bedside lamp.

Bonobos, apparently, make love, not war. They screw for hello; good-bye; I'm sad; I'm happy; I'm scared; I'll trade you nooky for a banana; Let's fight—No, let's *fuck*. It's not real fucking, mostly, since often there is no insertion of anything anywhere. It's more a frantic humping or mons rubbing or penis fencing between any gender at any time, regardless of age or familial connection. There's also plenty of French kissing, oral sex, and Kama Sutra angles. The only taboo seems to be grown sons and their mothers. This is quite a relief to Natalie, who at that moment wishes she could pluck her son from the desert and hoist him up into a thick forest canopy where he can hide out and be safe. Until she reads that the bonobos' habitat in the Congo is endangered by war and the militia is hunting them to near extinction for their meat. She pictures sweaty soldiers leaning over the dead animals. Diamonds spill from their shirt pockets and nestle like eggs in the chimps' fur.

At supper Natalie chooses vegetarian lasagna. She's sitting at a round table with her class. *Dinner with the author*, it's called, though even here the students do most of the talking. Across the table sits Hannah Pasqual, scraping the red sauce layer by layer from her meaty lasagna and eating only the abraded pasta. Natalie's heart begins thrashing again. She has no idea what to say tomorrow at the end of Hannah's workshop when the class inevitably looks to the leader for ultimate judgment. *Terrific vocabulary. Lovely sensory details. Your descriptions are phenomenal.* All hackneyed drivel that adds up to nothing.

Beside Hannah sits Peggy, spearing the cherries from her dish of canned fruit cocktail, savoring them as if they are forbidden fruit. Something twinges in Natalie's belly, or lower down actually, where two plum-shaped buds once nested.

That evening there is an open mic for the students in the lodge cantina, a low-ceilinged, square room with a laminate dance floor in the very center like a boxing ring, tables and booths surrounding it. Still sleep-deprived, Natalie avoids the crowded faculty booth in the corner and slumps at a table for two beside the only window, half open, a faint breeze sneaking in. A dangling plant overhead in a macramé sling strokes the top of her head, a soothing caress. Natalie gazes outside at the gentle desert hill rising up, the craggy fissures and bends of pink earth, the low hedge of thorny green shrubs, the impressionistic splotches of yellow. The most striking image of all, of course, are the saguaros looking like alert sentries on watch, or soldiers marching toward battle on the other side of the hill. *Stay down*, she mutters to Nathan, terrified of the insurgents who know this terrain far better than he, every cave, every boulder to hide behind. But there are so many in Nathan's unit that she can't count them all. *Cover each other*, she prays. The gentle breeze picks up force, shuddering the green shrubs, the saguaro, which bend in the wind, looking so much like penises that now Natalie can't think of them as anything else, thank God. This isn't a battlefield at all and she wonders if after the sun sets the cacti will uproot themselves and engage in their own massive games of penis-fencing. She can't stifle the bubble of laughter caught in her throat that bursts out of her mouth like a shriek.

"What's so funny?" Beth says, swaggering toward her with a pitcher of margaritas and two oversized glasses.

Natalie points at the prickly erections which gets her giggling again. "Penises," is all she can sputter.

"Why the hell do you think I moved out here?" Beth says, as if she gets the full joke, or one of her own.

"Are you sure you don't want to sit with them?" Natalie says, nodding toward the rest of the faculty yammering away in their booth.

"Be serious," Beth says. "They're only here tonight because it's in their contract." She sits and natters on about her new life in Tucson, which sounds amazingly similar to her old lives in Boston, Seattle, Denver—except for the wardrobe and topography. Natalie once again wonders where she might relocate if she decided to call it quits. All of it. James. Her blabbering mother. Just pick up and leave with no forwarding address. Forget the books and computer and photo albums—except Nathan's, she would have to take his. Someplace warm, she thinks, where she can grow lemons.

Natalie drinks urgently as the sun slides behind that hill, the penises just black silhouettes now. She thinks she hears them whispering to each other: *Get ready.*

The room dims and a waitress moves from table to table lighting red candles in chunky fishnet-covered glass bowls, the kind Natalie hasn't seen in decades.

Students congregate on the dance floor where a microphone has been set up. They pore over the signup sheet, looking lost and disorganized. Several are talking at once, stepping on each other's words: *Dory should go after Emily and then Matt. No! It should go girl-boy-girl-boy-girl-boy.* All that finger pointing and list snatching. Hannah Pasqual slides in and scuffs toward the melee with her notebook, head down, bumping into people and tables because she's still madly scribbling.

Natalie presses her back against the wicker chair, the twined cane squeaking.

The microphone wails and Brad from Natalie's workshops says: "Is someone supposed to kick this thing off?"

"Shit," Beth says. "That would be me."

She pushes out of her chair and makes her way forward still clutching her margarita, ready to allay the students' fears and pull order out of chaos. It all comes so naturally to Beth, Natalie thinks. This mothering, this taking care of minor conference nuisances: misplaced manuscripts, forgotten medications, lost cell phones, dietary restrictions.

A clump of conferees enter, Peggy-of-the-plums among them. All women, mostly middle-aged and older, some arm-in-arm. They take the last empty booth directly across from Natalie, on the other side of the dance floor. She watches them scoot across the vinyl bench, their shorts and skirts sliding up their dimpled thighs, hints of white underwear flashing. They don't appear to mind as they snuggle together shoulder to shoulder so that everyone can fit.

Very bonobo, Natalie thinks, recalling the last bit she read about the chimps who often exhibit selfless tendencies. They are a matriarchal society. All that lesbian sex bonds them together as a unified front. The males are less aggressive with each other or outsiders under this gynocentric hierarchy, preferring the good sex they can find at home to senseless war. They are also more tolerant of the children, just like James, who was not only tolerant but absolutely smitten with their son. Totally gaga. Natalie doesn't know which one of them was more demolished when they discovered there would be no more children.

The microphone sputters and whines as Beth grips it by the neck and practically swallows the head. "To all who are about to die, we salute you!"

"Hear, hear," one of the bonobo women answers.

Beth starts to make her way back to the table but she's yanked off course by one of the wait people. Another fire to douse.

A buxom girl takes the microphone and says her name is Babette.

She starts reading too loudly, hands gesticulating wildly, a 1950s floor show with red lipstick, big side-swept hair, over-sized jewelry and erupting cleavage. *A man's woman*, Natalie thinks, the appraisal confirmed when she scours the room and watches the older men at the faculty booth unpeel Babs with their eyes. They don't hear a word of her story and neither does Natalie.

Brad is next and his reading is surprisingly timid after all that chest-puffing. Natalie can barely hear him, nor can anyone else, especially now that the faculty are engaged in their own conversation which increases steadily in volume. Beth laughs from a distant corner, having been sidetracked by a cute bartender. Natalie watches Beth's mouth, the lusty way she guzzles her drink. She keeps looking over at Natalie and holding up a finger as if to say: *I'll be there in a minute! Just a minute!*

Take your time, Natalie mouths back, relieved, because she genuinely wants to hear the students though with each brave soul the audience becomes less attentive. Except for the bonobo women who try to shush the unruly rabble so they can better hear the youngsters taking the stage, one after another, like so many grandchildren reciting memory verses: *I think that I shall never see . . . .* But the rest of the mob has their own urgent ramblings to spill, whole dictionaries worth. Natalie's eyes bounce from booth to table, all those yammering jaws pouring out words that nobody hears. Like her mother back home, who desperately needs for someone to just pull up a chair and acknowledge her stories that have been gestating for such a very long time.

Eventually Hannah Pasqual makes her way toward the mic and Natalie wants to take in every syllable, every pregnant pause. The din is too loud so she tries to read Hannah's lips, such a little girl mouth. And then the words don't matter because her hand grips the microphone and it is surprisingly small, such tiny fingers. Hannah tries to raise her voice to compete, but she can't, so she stops talking and looks over at the oblivious faculty. The bonobo follow her gaze and bare their teeth. "Will you all be quiet?" Peggy shouts to no avail. And then Natalie realizes that the faculty are glaring at her, talking behind their hands, eyes on fire as they no doubt wonder if, after all this time, she has anything important left to say.

Natalie looks at Hannah casting her pearls. Genuine, beautiful, significant pearls scattering on the floor like pebbles that nobody wants. Hannah reads on but her arms begin fluttering like bird wings preparing for flight. She steals peeks of the faculty sharpening their knives, and Bev at the bar too busy flirting with the bartender.

A tap on the widow and Natalie knows who it is, a cluster of shadowy figures calling to her: *It's time.*

"Listen," Natalie says.

A few heads pivot her way, but the noise doesn't subside.

"Listen!" she says more boldly.

Hannah looks at her with that little girl mouth, her trembling almond-nailed fingers, knees beginning to buckle, one hand curled as if she's clutching a plum too tightly, bruising its tender flesh.

Without forethought Natalie stands and marches forward, nudging tables and chairs as she makes her way onto the dance floor. Hannah's eyes widen as Natalie approaches, knocks the microphone completely over, and grips her in a bear hug so tight it's as if Natalie is hugging herself, and maybe she is. Hannah squirms at first, then her rigid body relaxes, a sigh slips from her mouth as if it's been bottled up since birth. Natalie wants to whisper something into the girl's ear, some important gift, but even now, especially now, there are no words, so she does the only thing that feels right, she presses her lips against Hannah's and holds them there, just holds them there firmly, a kiss Hannah accepts without resistance for two seconds, three, as all sound dies away and they stand there bathed in such delicious quiet after so much noise.

All eyes are on them, Beth's too, though her mouth is agape. But Natalie doesn't care because she can hear the breeze slipping through the window, seeking her out, twining its airy tendrils around her arms and legs, lifting her up to whisk through the open window and out into the sky. Down below the Saguaro are frolicking, banging and bumping, not a soldier among them, spilling their milky seed across the desert floor and who knows what will take root, a twenty-acre peach orchard, perhaps, where Natalie's son can rest in the shade. She floats above it all, but something begins to weigh her down, her satchel strapped across her shoulder, dangling toward earth. She reaches in to lighten her burden so she can really take flight and pulls out her own seeds to scatter: lemons and plums; To-Do lists and diamonds; a tangle of knotted-up letters: f-l-u-k-e; her mother's voice— finally free; and pages from a novel Natalie will never finish which scatter like paper birds in the wind.

Counting Backwards

There are 732 floor tiles in this corridor—at least from the elevator to the VISITORS NOT ALLOWED BEYOND THIS POINT sign. 12 light switches. 28 doorknobs. 3 NO SMOKING signs. 7 moonrise-over-the-ocean framed prints. And 13 visitors' chairs (mauve and blue plaid) including mine. It is 26 steps from the elevator to Chrissy's door. Of course, I wear a 13 work boot and have a long stride. I don't know how many steps from inside the door to Chrissy. It's 527 days since I've been in there and I wasn't counting when I was.

And I wasn't always counting.

The first month I just watched. 18 hours a day. From this chair.

Douglas the Thursday Floor Waxer is minimally retarded. He asked me to teach him how to flirt with the respiratory therapist who wears rose scrubs and a turquoise crucifix in her left ear. I told him to do something nice for her. Now he polishes an extra shiny path from the R.T. doorway to the cafeteria, one of her favorite routes.

The Vending Machine Refiller says, "Ed, the reason the mini-donuts are always the first to go is because they're the biggest package for the money." I say it is because people like the third knob from the left. It's a comfortable knob. Well-worn. People need small comforts here. He says, "People need vending nourishment to sustain them through these ordeals." I say they need motion. Body movements. Insert. Pull. Unwrap. Eat. Makes them feel like they're adding something to the cause. Sending out healthy sparks that just might make it down the hall, under the door, and into the tube of their Somebody Special.

I think it's a built-in function of humans to count. Money. Scores. Faults. Heartbeats. Heartbeats are all Chrissy's got now. I'm counting everything else. I'm hoping someday I'll hit the right number and a jackpot of forgiveness will spill out all over me.

Christine Salir was an attorney with Wade, Brock, and Rowe. She drove a cherry red Impulse and carried an ostrich-skin briefcase. Her town house was on Seawall Boulevard. I walk by there on Sundays on my way to the pier. Nice. Red brick and wrought iron. Two men live there now. In the mornings they wear kimonos and drink coffee out of tiny china cups. They also read *The Galveston News* if I don't get there first.

I like to go down to the water early and listen to lapping. Lapping is the only thing I don't count. Sometimes I bring Douglas the Thursday Floor Waxer with me. He is learning to fish. He wants to catch a big one for his R.T.

It is 1.2 miles from my trailer to St. Stephen's. 2.3 from the pier. Dr. Castinoli insisted I come 1 less day. He said, "I don't think it's healthy, all this counting." So now I'm down to 6 days with Chrissy.

But I'm not the only one down. Mr. Salir is down to Saturdays. I don't know about Mrs. Salir. I think she's down to nothing.

Mr. Salir takes 32 steps to get to Chrissy's room. It used to be 18. 23. 27. Now it's 32. If he remembers, he won't look at me when he passes. But sometimes he forgets and nods a glazed stare. I remember 1 time when his eyes were grateful and he pumped my hands and cried. Then Dr. Castinoli called him into a corner to talk in whispers and he cried some more but was no longer grateful.

47 minutes is Mr. Salir's average visit with Chrissy. I try to imagine what goes on in that sterilized cell. It is very difficult. I'm not sure what she looks like now. I know their faces change. He will smooth her hair and talk in a quiet voice. A daddy's voice to a 38-year-old woman. She will lay fetal and suck her tongue. He will unpack and pack the blue duffel he always carries. Underclothes and nightgowns. What else could it be? And then he takes his 32 steps away from her. 3 minutes down the elevator if it stops on all floors.

Every third Wednesday comes Dwayne. He circles me like I circle Chrissy. Dwayne and I were paramedics together. We logged 792 runs. Mostly car wrecks. Chrissy's was the last—for me, at least. He used to say, "You did what you thought was right, Ed." Now he just says, "When you coming back?" We both know the answer, but he's a good friend to keep up the pretense.

Sometimes I ask the nurses about Chrissy. I don't know why, because they always answer: The same. Chrissy has been here 530 days and she is still: The same. She will never be anything other than: The same.

I can count 13 blocks to the pier from this hospital window. It's 8 stories up. The east wing. A nice view. I can also watch flashing ambulances nudge their way through blacktopped maze. I remember that pacing depression Dwayne and I used to get when we hadn't had a run for awhile. Then the adrenaline-pumping, temple-throbbing, better-than-coke rush when we were on our way. Sirens spinning. Alive or dead. God is here. And then the heavy sleep of exhaustion.

Sally has sent me 17 letters—the last 3 postmarked Albuquerque. Sally is my ex-wife. 12 months ago she said she was tired of me counting everything but pay stubs. She then collected the savings account, address book, baby, and started running from relative to relative, state to state. She's also sent 2 telegrams and 1 pick-me-up bouquet. I still have the rainbow vase, and somewhere in a letter S encyclopedia is a dried white daisy. S for Salir, not Sally.

Chrissy has 1 sister, Janine. Janine is 31 and the only Salir who will talk to me, which is when she flies in from Seattle on Christmas and the Fourth of July. "I can't stand my parents any longer than that," she says. We always go to the hospital atrium and sit on a wooden bench where Janine can smoke. Virginia Slims. She burns them down to the filter and lights up another right away. 4-pack-a-day habit, at least. Smoking got her fired from a waitressing job at Denny's. Ashes in the bean soup. Then she worked in a photo hut in the parking lot of some mall. "I can smoke all day long and I get all the reprints I want."
Last Christmas Janine brought a photo album of when Chrissy was small. She was a blue-eyed baby. Cantaloupe bald with pudgy legs. Janine can't go into Chrissy's hospital room either. Reprints will have to do.

Douglas the Thursday Floor Waxer lives with 7 other limited men. They all work and pay rent—things I used to do. I went home with him for supper 1 night. The house was extremely clean and they had a Creole cook named Simone. She stirred a thick smell all through the house and some of it spilled out onto the patio where I was picking dead leaves from a Wandering Jew.

Simone was strict with those people—with me. Went around the table and made us each tell what we'd done productive that day. I said: "There were 53 red cars in the hospital parking lot today if you count all shades."

Dr. Castinoli is becoming concerned about my numbers. "Seventeen notebooks are enough," he says. But I say 17 notebooks, 2700 pages, 178,500 lines, 900,000 words are not enough when it's all Chrissy's got left. "Ed," Dr. Castinoli says, "she'll never see them." This is when I start counting sprinkler heads in the ceiling. Cracks in the floor tile. Gum wads under the chair (usually pink).

When I'm not at the hospital or the pier I'm selling blood, collecting cans, bottles, metal, rubber. It's how I pay for groceries and notebooks and pens. I have no phone, and the trailer is a freebie in exchange for the title: *24-Hour Maintenance Man* on the sign out front. The inhabitants don't know I'm their fixit man. I act like a regular and shrug whenever there's a problem. "Haven't seen him," I say.

Sally's last letter was a plea. "The baby needs a father. Come soon," was all it read. I filed it in the El Producto box with my father's railroad watch and my mother's wedding ring inscribed: "Till death." When my parents died, they really died. 92 days apart.

Last July Janine said she had a new job, service station attendant. She burned down the photo hut. "Film is highly flammable," she said. We sat in the atrium and went over numbers. Last to first. As if by going backwards we could change the beginning. Keep Chrissy an extra 5 minutes at work. A phone call would have done it. A trip to the bathroom. A dead battery.

But her car started right up. Japanese cars are notorious for that. She drove up Seawall Boulevard in that pouring rain. Right on Rosenberg. Left on Mechanic. Crossed the railroad tracks. I imagine she could already see me coming in the ambulance. Lights flashing. Siren screaming. Yet here came Chrissy. She probably wondered where the emergency was. What it was. Train wreck? Heart attack? Never knowing. Never sensing. Then I hydroplaned. Skidded across the median. Practically drove right through Chrissy's windshield.

It is Sunday, pier day, but I'm walking the wrong way. I'm carrying my suitcase to Douglas's house, to Simone. The trailer lot owners found me out. When I get there I say, "There are 9 dog houses on Bayou Shore Drive and 3 of them have no dog attached." Simone says, "You can sleep on the couch. Put your things in Douglas's room." It feels right to live in this house where small triumphs mean so much.

Douglas finally caught that big fish for his R.T. and Simone cooked it up special. He tied an orange bow to the lid and brought it to the Thanksgiving party in the employee lounge. I got invited because I'm more regular than most of them. I brought a bag of red delicious apples that had fallen off a truck. The Vending Machine Refiller brought a shoe box full of expired Little Debbie's.

The R.T. was impressed with the fish and kissed Douglas right on the mouth.

Dr. Castinoli was at this party. He said, "Ed, I've got somebody I want you to talk to. I'll get you an appointment as soon as I can. No charge." I said, "Doctor, there are only 29 shopping days till Christmas, and there's 1 button missing from your left sleeve."

Douglas couldn't sleep that night.

I got 2 interesting pieces of mail today. The first was a threat from Sally. It seems she's met someone. Robert. She doesn't love him, but he's good with our daughter and he's an electrician. The second was an appointment card for Dr. Rebecca Warner, Psychiatrist, January 7 at 9:30 a.m.

Robert. Wonder why he doesn't go by Bob.

Simone makes me help her in the kitchen. It is how I earn my couch. "Peel them potatoes, boy. Take out this trash." We made boudin sausage last week. She let me add spices and stuff the casings. Boudin reminds me of nurses' legs. Rubbery pink flesh squeezed into white nylons.

Today Simone is deveining shrimp for filé gumbo. "Chicken gizzards in the roux," she says. "My secret." She pats a chair beside her. "Sit down help me, boy." Which I do. Simone is chewing on a sassafras root and thinking very hard. Finally she says it. "Some day you gonna run out of numbers, then where you gonna be?" Simone puts 32 medium shrimp and 2 pounds of kielbasa into her gumbo. But she doesn't let it go. "Why you doin' this? Not for that brain-dead girl." I stand up. "This your penance or your hell?" I start walking to the living room. "All penance got to end sometime, Ed."

Dwayne and I were at Tibbitt's Drive-Inn Hot Dog Stand where his aunt cooked the Secret Special Sauce. Dwayne told his friends we supplied the meat—the secret that made the sauce so special. Business was slow because of that rain. I was flirting with a curb girl. She was impressed with our uniforms and kept looking over my shoulder at the ambulance. I said, "Wanna go for a ride?" Her eyes lit like sparklers. "Let me punch out and get my purse!" Dwayne was mad. His curb girl said no. So off we went. The three of us in the ambulance in that pouring rain. I was driving.

Janine runs the 32 feet from the elevator and sort of trips into my arms. "My sentinel!" she says. "I can always count on you." Janine is drunk. "I can't wait to see your numbers, Ed. What's Chrissy been missing this year?" We both look down the hall in Chrissy's direction. Janine actually takes a lunging step forward. "Are . . . are you going to . . ." I try to say. "No. No-no-no," Janine says before falling into a chair. She raises a finger to her lips, "Shhhhh. Nobody even knows I'm here. Do you know? Do you know what she did? My mother? She repapered Chrissy's old room without even asking me! New carpet. New drapes. She calls it the *guest room* now. Can you believe it? So what will Chrissy do when she walks into her old room and it's not there?" She pauses, droops slowly to the left, and throws up into the plastic rhododendron.

I keep her fairly quiet on the bus. It is a 17 minute ride to the house with 4 stops. Douglas wants Janine to sleep in his bed. Simone says no, she'll share hers. Douglas is mad. He doesn't even drink his nightly warm milk with vanilla and cinnamon. Simone makes Janine sip this beige Creole drink. "It'll keep your stomach down," she says. Janine likes the bowling pin nativity scene set up by the tree. One of the guys painted it. Nobody ever asked him where he got the pins. Janine starts whispering about Chrissy's last Christmas. "She got everybody these fabulous lawyer gifts. Golf clubs and tiaras and stuff. Everybody oooooed and ahhhed." I can barely hear what she's saying. "She did it to show off. I hated her for that and told her so. Told her right to her face. That's the last thing I ever said to my sister: *I hate your guts.*" The words come out in a tangible cloud that hangs in the air for several minutes.

My curb girl started flipping switches and turning knobs. I didn't care. Dwayne didn't care. "Aren't you married, Ed?" she said. "Every other day," I said. "This is my other day." She laughed. She seemed to like that. Up ahead I could see the light at Tremont turn red. I flipped the siren and hit the gas. Those cars scrambled when they saw us. Everybody checked their rearviews. The curb girl sucked in her breath when we swerved into the oncoming lane to pass a truck. She didn't breathe until we were through the light and back on our side of the road. Then she burst out laughing and squeezed my knee. Goosebumps beaded on her arm. I chased red lights after that.

I like the Christmas tree at our house better than the hospital's. Simone only allows handmade ornaments on her tree. There is an assortment of nearly successful origami birds and dragons, popsicle stick sleds, crocheted wreathes, paper snowflakes, and unidentifiable dried macaroni wads dipped in red glitter. I strung together a length of flip tops from soda cans. Not too creative, but they reflect the lights real pretty. When Simone comes back from putting Janine to bed she says, "She is a very troubled girl, Ed. She's more troubled than you."

I received a first-ever letter from my daughter. Inside is a crayon drawing of a smiling flower. There is a teepee in the sky and a dog labeled "Ed" trots along the bottom edge. Ed. A conspicuously well-scrawled message runs up the side. "Mommy is marrying Robert on Cristmas day." Sally never could spell Christmas.

All the men at Simone's house wait patiently in line outside the bathroom door. Janine, this strange woman, is showering in their tub. Washing her naked body with their soap. It is astounding. Douglas has dibs on the soap.

When I count backwards it is not to stall Chrissy. It is to stall me. And I could have, very easily. Sally was feeling amorous that day. She wanted me to call in sick. "You need a vacation, Eddie. We both need a vacation. I'll take the baby over to Mom's." But I just wiped her off my arm and drove away. Marriage was not my solution, baby or not. God, why didn't I just stay home and make love to my wife?

When I think about life before Chrissy I think of the sun beating down. I see white hot concrete. A sidewalk. A slab for a three-bedroom rancher. A subdivision driveway. It is a dry, dry feeling that reminds me of soap operas in the middle of the day with the drapes closed. Of school crossings without children. Of a sightless dead bird on the side of the road.

Since Chrissy, I have been sitting in the rain. That's what I feel like. My clothes are always moist and clingy. The paper in my notebooks is damp. But I'm comfortable in this weather. I like pulling my clothes around me. Hiking up my collar. Shoving hands into pockets.

Janine is still at our house. 2 days and she hasn't called her parents. She hasn't had a cigarette either. House rules. Simone ground a bitter herb for Janine to rub into her gums. Janine swears it works. Now she sits in the kitchen all day long peeling my potatoes.

"She wants you back, your wife," Simone says. My daughter's crayon drawing is taped to the refrigerator. "You are a lucky man, Ed. Now let's see how smart you are."

The ambulance flew thirty feet and landed on all fours. The curb girl had a slight concussion. Dwayne had minor lacerations and a sprained wrist. Me, not a bump, not a drop of blood. Dwayne said, "Ed, you are a lucky, lucky man." Then we saw Chrissy's Impulse.

She ate the steering wheel pretty good but I couldn't get at her. Every door buckled. Every window jammed. And she was turning that gray upholstery maroon. I was pounding-kicking-hitting, but she couldn't hear a thing. Dwayne called Jaws of Life but that was too slow. I grabbed a bumper trying to crack that windshield like a piñata. Nothing. It was five minutes. Ten minutes. Fifteen damn minutes before they got there and another five to pop the door. They figured dead-at-the-scene, but I ventilated and compressed like a maniac. Dwayne tried to pull me off her, "It's too late, man." But I didn't listen. "She's gone, Ed. Let it go!" I pushed him off, "Like hell she is!"

Then I got it. A pulse. A breath.

It was still raining when Mr. and Mrs. Salir arrived at the hospital. They were soaking. Mr. Salir wore fake control. "Nobody could find us we were at the ballet we just got the message on our machine." Dwayne introduced himself and pointed to me. Mr. Salir came over and shook my hand. He didn't know any better. He thought I just saved his daughter's life. Dr. Castinoli walked in. He'd put a lab coat over his scrubs but the blood still seeped through. He pulled the Salirs into a corner, sat them down. They talked for awhile. Dr. Castinoli shook his head and Mrs. Salir cried and cried and cried.

"How's the service station job going?" I finally ask Janine. "Gasoline is highly flammable, too," she says.

I talked to Mr. Salir today. Sort of. It was lunchtime and I waited for the elevator in front of a hungry crowd of housekeeping staff. When the doors slid open there he was. This wasn't his regular day and I froze. So did he. But the crowd pushed me inside, right into Chrissy's father, and I knocked him to the ground. I bent to help him, but he swatted my hands away. "Don't!" he said, and kept swatting even after I'd stepped back outside. Housekeeping stood and stared at this man sitting in the middle of the elevator. He looked up into my eyes, "Don't you dare help me." He held me with a hard stare, but before the doors hissed shut I said, "I'm sorry." The elevator jolted and hummed down toward the lobby. I yelled after it, "I'm sorry!"

I don't have many belongings, but I had a few things scattered around Douglas's room. My Producto box. Rainbow vase. My daughter's teething ring—I keep meaning to send that. This morning I noticed all of my possessions had migrated to the coffee table. "Just dusting," Simone said and went in the kitchen to make beignets with Janine.

When Sally made it to the hospital she had streaks of mascara running down her cheeks. Dwayne told her everything—including the curb girl. But Sally just hugged my neck and kissed my face hard. A cement sun beating down on my rain.

It was my third visit to see Chrissy since the wreck. Red and purple swelled out around gauze and tape. I was leaning over the bed rail when Mrs. Salir walked in. She stopped short when she saw me, then stepped forward very slowly, very deliberately and slapped my face as hard as she could. Then she slapped it again, turned around, and walked out.

At 7:30 p.m. Simone sits us all down for Christmas Eve dinner. Deep fried turkey injected with peanut oil. Douglas gets to carve and he gives Janine the first slice. All the men like having Janine in the house. A woman who is not Simone. They all have last minute gifts for her under the tree. A Quality Inn shower cap. Baggie full of

M&Ms. A glass doorknob. Douglas bought her a black pair of panties.

Simone gives me a straw hat with a red bandanna. "I hear the sun beat down hard in Albuquerque." She clasps my face in her burning Creole hands. "Tomorrow wedding bells gonna ring, dear boy, unless you are smart as I think." Then she goes to the bedroom and softly shuts the door.

Janine and I look at each other from opposite ends of the couch. Still my couch. "Have you called your parents yet? I mean, you're flying back to Seattle tomorrow, right?"

She crosses and recrosses her legs. "Well, see, I was going to fly back but, I was thinking, that is, and Simone agrees, maybe it would be better if I stayed here for awhile. It's not like I have a job or anything to go back to."

"Oh, and Simone agrees."

"Well, not directly, but I can tell that it would be all right if I just sort of—stayed."

There is this enormous pause for a minute and the air becomes too thick to breathe.

I stand up too abruptly and clap my hands on my thighs. "I guess you've pretty much got dibs on the couch." She stands up fast, too, and shoves her plane ticket into my shirt pocket. I was used to her whisper, but I still had to stoop.

". . . that maybe you were going to go back to your wife. At least that's what she's hoping you'll do. I thought you could trade in my ticket to Seattle for a flight to Albuquerque."

Her eyes were so hopeful for me that I could not possibly have refused.

I scoop my 17 notebooks from the coffee table. This stack represents 496 days' worth of adding and multiplying and estimating. It also represents 496 days of my life. I count them as well-spent days. Janine's eyebrows arch when I hand them over, then she holds them to her chest and nods. I'm about to turn away, but I stop and reach into my back pocket for the appointment card. Dr. Rebecca Warner, Psychiatrist, January 7, 9:30 a.m. "Here," I say. "You better take this, too." I think maybe Janine needs this house of small triumphs more than I do. "And watch out for Douglas."

Janine stands in front of the yellow porch light so I cannot see her face. As I get into the cab she trickles a stream of white cement words across the yard. "Good luck in Albuquerque, Ed."

"Albuquerque," I say. But in my mind I am already pulling up my collar to the contentment of Seattle rain, with long days of nothing but deep-fisted pockets and the lapping of wave after wave after wave.

Crystal City

Lucky Baby snatches *The Tormenta Falls Herald* from her husband's grip. "Let me see!" she says, peeling off the rubber band, frantically flipping pages with pudgy ink-stained fingers until she knocks her orange juice into her Cheerios.

"Calm down," Joe says, mopping up the mess with the dish towel tucked into his Wranglers. "It'll be in there."

"I know it will," she snipes, tossing out the sports section, classifieds, comics, until she finds the local and scans page one, two, three. "Here it is!" she shouts, folding the paper to highlight the 4 x 4 column announcement that reads: *Lucky Baby Turns 58! Happy Birthday to our Cowboy Bob Show Girl!* Beside it is a grainy halftone of Lucky Baby and Cowboy Bob taken in 1947 when she was just five years old. Cowboy Bob squats beside her, ten-gallon hat perched way back on his head to expose the golden forelock—his TV trademark. He poses cheek-to-cheek with Lucky Baby who sports slick black ponytails.

Baby hugs the paper to her chest. "They remembered," she coos, squeezing her eyes shut, little lower lip quivering.

"Course they did," Joe says, patting his wife's hair, the shiny black ball of it knotted at the base of her neck, the half-inch silver roots that will be touched up this morning.

"I wish they used the other picture, though," she says, referring to the one taken during her second season, sitting on top of the Steinway, little Mary Jane's gleaming, frilly dress flouncing over a scratchy slip. Her head tipped to the side. That was her pose, the one she'd angle into after she and Cowboy Bob crooned "The Yellow Rose of Texas" into each other's eyes at the end of each show. That way the home audience could see the genuine affection between their local celebrity and the darling girl rescued from Crystal City, the Internment Camp built twenty miles west to hold German-Italian-Japanese Americans, and German-Italian-Japanese *Latin* Americans. The latter—JLAs, like Baby's family, shipped up by their Central and South American governments at the United States' request.

But Lucky Baby isn't concerned with all that. She has brisket to marinate, jumbo shrimp to peel, potatoes to mash for her birthday supper not ten hours away.

"Did you call about the cake?" she asks.

Joe sets a fresh bowl of cereal before her. "Course I did. And remember, when everyone gets here, don't say anything about the—"

"I won't," Baby says.

"Not a peep to your beauty parlor gals either."

"I *won't*," Baby says. "Though I don't know what's the big deal."

"People get jealous over less," he says, handing her a vitamin. "Now swallow this."

Joe pushes open the door to Lila's Beauty Spot, tarnished bell over the door tinkling as Lucky Baby sidles in. "Happy Birthday!" Lila calls from the third chair.

"Happy birthday!" yodels Bettyanne, another regular, from under the dryer, tags of foil crimped into her hair flapping under the heat.

Lila points to an assortment of bottles and tubes. "I've got everything ready," she says, patting the chair with a trembly, liver-spotted hand. At seventy-seven, Lila shouldn't hold a scissors to anyone's head.

Lucky Baby slides up into #3, her feet barely touching the floor.

"I'll be back in an hour," Joe says, backing out the door.

"Don't forget to pick up the ice cream!" Baby calls.

"I won't," Joe says, the door shutting behind him.

"Or the candles!"

"Got it," Joe mouths through the glass. He clicks an imaginary lock over his lips for secrecy, and then he is gone.

Baby pulls a tissue from her bra and wipes the back of her neck. "It's like a sauna out there," she says. "I wish to God it would rain."

"You and me both," Lila says. She fastens a vinyl cape around Baby's neck and starts combing, yanking at uncooperative tangles.

"Ow!" Baby says, and "Jeez!"

"Sorry," says Lila. "I'm a little nervous. I want your hair to look perfect for your sisters' visit. Got everything ready? "

"Almost," Baby says, mentally checking off her To-Do list, staring at advertising posters taped to the wall. Girls with crew cuts. Boys with frosted hair. When did men get so prissy, she wonders. Not like her Joe who still Brylcreems his hair every morning before snapping on his shirt. His skin leathery from all those years of wildcatting. Oh, the stories he has told her about drilling oil wells in Alaska and the Gulf of Mexico and Saudi Arabia. But he is more than just muscles. He is book smart, too, and she married him just in time so he could make sense of all the legal forms Baby got in the mail during the initial redress campaign in 1988. She certainly couldn't decipher all those pages of USE BLACK INK ONLY, SIGN ON THIS LINE, INITIAL HERE. Twelve years later Joe's knowledge is coming in handy again. That's devotion, Baby thinks and then she reminds herself to keep quiet, don't utter a word.

"I know you'll be glad to see Isabel," Lila says about Baby's middle sister. "But I never thought Carmen would set foot on Texas soil again."

Baby nibbles the inside of her cheek. "Me either."

"Course who could blame her," Lila says, eyes rolling up to the ceiling, rewinding the years. "I remember when Crystal City was built," she says, and Baby settles in for the spiel she's heard a million times. "How it was supposed to be top secret hush-hush, but Daddy drove the whole family over one Saturday and parked as close as he could get. We sat in the car and listened to hammering and sawing, saw towers and barracks being built, rolls of barbed wire. Daddy shook his head and said: *Hysteria. Everybody's got the hysteria.*"

"Yep," Baby says, but she stopped listening. She's reconsidering her outfit for tonight: shorts or skirt. Spaghetti straps or sleeves.

"Wonder why Carmen's coming back now?"

"I don't know," Baby says.

Baby looks in the mirror and frowns at the fan of wrinkles around her eyes, the sagging jowls. In her mind she's still the porcelain-skinned doll doting mothers dressed their Caucasian daughters up to look like. Now she's an old woman, but Carmen is fourteen years older. Seventy-two. They haven't seen each other in fifty-four years. Not in person, anyway. Baby has seen snapshots sent from Los Angeles where Carmen and Isabel moved after the war. Carmen and Isabel standing up to their knees in the Pacific Ocean. Wearing Mickey Mouse ears at Disneyland. Dressed in kimonos at some Japanese tea house. Baby wondered why they wanted to do a thing like that. They were born in Peru, for God's sake. Their first language was Spanish. But there they were, holding up tiny tea cups like they'd been doing it their entire lives. And they did look authentic with their heavy lidded eyes and coifed, charcoal hair. Now Carmen is coming, probably to talk her ear off about redress and retribution and the upcoming Day of Remembrance, the anniversary of FDR's Executive Order 9066 which ultimately sent thousands of Japanese Americans and JLAs to internment camps.

That's ancient history as far as Baby is concerned. She is an American, born on Texas soil in the Crystal City hospital to a mother who didn't survive the delivery. Raised in Tormenta Falls, a close-knit town that claimed her as their very own poster child of goodwill. They would show the world something about Texas manners, about hospitality and forgiveness.

"I'm nervous," Baby says aloud though she didn't mean to.

Lila parts Baby's hair and squirts on dye. "About seeing Carmen? What for?"

Baby opens her mouth but the words won't come, and she doesn't trust her rusty memories. She has to rely on stories told during Isabel's yearly visits about how Carmen wanted to take Lucky Baby away from Cowboy Bob, from Tormenta Falls, from smiling crowds and photographers who yelled: "Say cheese!" at grocery store and car lot openings.

But Lucky Baby didn't want to move to the west coast with her frowning older sister in her sad black dress. She wanted to live with Joan and Wally Adkins, a solid Baptist couple who opened their arms to Lucky Baby and gave her her very own room and a closet full of starched gingham dresses.

"Have you heard from Cowboy Bob?" Bettyanne calls from under the dryer.

"I will. Probably in today's mail. He hasn't missed a birthday or Christmas yet."

"How's he like Florida?" Lila asks.

"He loves it," Baby says. It's a guess. He never signs anything but his name though his signature markedly changed decades back, an anomaly Baby attributes to rheumy eyes or medication or the tremor of old age.

The bell over the door sounds and in bursts two tow-headed boys followed by Emily Crockett, looking wilted from the record-breaking temperature. "Don't run!" she screams at her visiting grandsons, her shrill voice piercing Baby's eardrums. "Go sit in those chairs and keep still!" Emily clips across the linoleum in her sling-back shoes, ankles thick from edema.

Lila frowns at the daisy wall clock. "Birtie's running late this morning, but I'm sure she'll be in shortly for your wash and set."

"No hurry." Emily tugs a lavender envelope from her purse and offers it to Baby. "I got you a card."

Baby pulls her hand out from under the vinyl cloak. "Thank you," she says, eyes glistening.

The two boys fidget and wrestle in the chairs until the chubby one pops up and runs to Lucky Baby.

"Are you her?" he asks.

"What?" Baby says.

"From the TV. Grandma told us we might see a celebrity today."

Baby sits up straighter and cocks her head to the side, smiling. "Yes I am."

The boy puffs out his cheeks and peels: "Tanjoubi omedetou!"

Baby scrunches her eyebrows. "Pardon?"

"Tanjoubi omedetou!" he repeats. "Happy birthday in Japanese. I looked it up on the Internet."

Lila's and Bettyanne's eyeballs meet as Baby pulls her mouth into a tight line. "I don't speak Japanese."

"But Grandma said you were—"

Emily grabs his forearm. "Hush up, now."

"But you said she was—"

"Never mind what I said," Emily scolds, yanking him to the door. "Come on Wayne," she says to the other boy. "We'll come back when Bertie is in," Emily says, face crimson, and the door hisses closed behind them.

Baby's jugular pulses on the side of her neck. "I speak English," she says.

"I know," Lila says, frantically globbing on dye.

At 4:45 Baby taps the lime Jell-O mold from its ring. "The grapes sunk to the bottom again," she says. "And the pecans."

Joe pulls his barbeque tongs from under the sink. "Nobody'll notice."

"How are you supposed to keep them from sinking, huh? I'd like to know that." Baby jabs the sad gelatinous blob. "Did you check the mail again?"

"Yes," Joe says. "It's still not here."

"It's never been this late before. You think something happened?"

"People get sick. Trucks break down."

"Then they get a new truck, a substitute driver. Don't they know people need their mail? People rely on their mail?"

Baby bangs her foot against the dishwasher just as a car turns into the driveway. "It's them," Baby says, foot frozen.

"Sounds like," says Joe. Suddenly both break into a run to peer out the front window. Isabel is behind the wheel and Baby strains to make out the figure in the passenger seat. There she is. Carmen. The door opens and she slides out, looking so fragile in her gauzy yellow dress with saucer-sized flowers embroidered around the hem. Red handbag over one shoulder. Navy blue Keds. Her hair is silver white, cut short-short, making her neck look so thin, too thin to hold up the three-inch half moon earrings dangling from her lobes.

"Not what I expected," Baby says.

"What'd you expect?"

"Not that," Baby says.

Baby watches Carmen stretch from side to side, undoubtedly stiff from the long trip. She refuses to fly since that turbulent trip she made to visit their brother in Nagasaki last year.

Joe straightens Baby's collar and wipes a lipstick smudge from her cheek. "Remember," he says, "not a word."

"Right," Baby says, her eyes fastened on Carmen who, though no longer in a sad black dress, still wears a prominent frown.

Baby opens the front door. "You made it!" she calls, overly chipper.

"Finally," Isabel says, flapping her shirt to let air in.

"Dios mío," Carmen says. "Hace mucho calor aquí."

"Sí," Isabel says, fanning her face with a road map.

"Un horno," Carmen adds, looking at Baby as though she is responsible for the weather.

Isabel walks to Baby, arms wide for a hug. She looks good, Baby thinks, in her scooter skirt and sandals, permed hair. Still so youthful and thin at 68. Baby runs a hand over her own bulging belly, self-conscious.

"It's good to see you," Isabel says. "You too, Joe," she adds, offering him a hug.

Joe pats her on the back. "How was the trip?"

Isabel rolls her eyes. "Thirty hours in a car in this heat wave. You tell me."

"I told you to fly," Carmen says. "I could have taken the train." Carmen turns her eye on Baby, who edges behind her husband.

"Let me see you," Carmen directs.

Baby comes forward and they stand face to face, eyes locked, not knowing whether to hug or shake hands.

"This is our Baby," Isabel says. "Didn't she turn out fine?"

"Sí," Carmen nods, steely-eyed. The three sisters stand in an uncomfortable ring and Baby wonders how they will possibly survive this visit. Sweat trickles down her back and she searches for something, anything, to say.

"Well let's get you all settled," Joe finally says, escorting the ladies inside.

Joe hauls the suitcases to the spare room as the women gravitate to the fireplace—the mantle and paneled wall covered with Cowboy Bob Show memorabilia: photos and newspaper clippings, a tiny dress on a hanger, a bronzed pair of size four Mary Jane's, a golden statue that reads: Best Local Children's Show, 1950. Baby steps back to let her sisters take it all in.

Carmen leans close to one of the newspaper clippings. "I guess you really were a big star back then."

"Still is," Joe says, returning. "Look at this," he says, pointing to a wall of photographs taken over the years: Lucky Baby with Dale Evans, Soupy Sales, Willard Scott. "And these," Joe says, fanning out an eight-inch stack of birthday cards. "From all over the world," he says. "See? Canada and Oregon and Milwaukee. Everybody still loves Lucky Baby."

"Course they do," Isabel says. "Carmen didn't mean anything by it."

Carmen picks up a photo of Baby in her high school graduation gown flanked by a middle-aged couple both wearing horn-rimmed glasses. "Who's this?"

Baby looks at the couple in the frame, the man's arm clamped around Baby's shoulders, the woman wearing an orchid corsage. "My parents."

"¿Cómo?" Carmen says, voice an octave too high. She holds the picture inches from her face.

"Her *foster* parents," Isabel says.

"Oh," Carmen says, banging the photo back down.

Everyone looks at the floor, the sculpted brown carpet.

"Why don't you show Carmen the back yard?" Joe says.

"Yes!" Baby says, relieved. She walks them out onto the back patio and waves at the scalloped gardens with prickly pear cactus, the grape arbor. The old water pump Joe converted into a fountain. The detached garage that houses Joe's '56 Corvette, his *real* wife, Baby teases. The showpiece, of course, is the hot tub and cedar sauna. Baby centers Carmen before it and waits for her praise.

Carmen hugs her red purse. "Isn't Texas a little hot for a sauna?"

Baby frowns. "Not in the winter," she says. "Joe and I come out here late at night when it's cool."

"Seems a waste if you can't use it year round," Carmen says. "And even then only at night."

Baby cracks her knuckles, one mighty pop after another.

"It's nice," Isabel says. "I used it last time I was here."

"Must have cost a pretty penny," Carmen adds. "Probably took every bit of that $20,000—"

Isabel nudges her sister. "Shhh!" she says. "¡Tranquila!"

Baby's left eyebrow twitches. "We only used part of it for that." She points toward Joe's garage. "Most of it went for the—"

"Hush!" Joe says. "They aren't interested in our finances. Now you all go inside where it's cool and I'll start up the barbeque." He stomps over to the gas grill and heaves up the lid as the ladies go back inside.

Carmen and Isabel settle on the sofa across from the picture window while Baby fetches sweet tea from the kitchen. She mimics: "Seems like a waste of money if you can't use it year round."

Joe comes in the back door. "I told you to keep your mouth shut."

Baby plunks ice into three glasses. "I didn't say anything."

Joe grabs the brisket from the refrigerator. "Not yet, but one thing leads to another and pretty soon you'll blow the whole deal."

"I won't blow anything," she says, setting the glasses on a plastic tray next to a port-wine cheese ball surrounded by Triscuits. "And I still don't see what's the big deal."

"You wouldn't," Joe says, banging out the back door.

When Baby brings the tea and hors d'oeuvres to her sisters, Isabel is close to Carmen's face, furiously whispering.

"Okay," Carmen says to Isabel. "Okay!"

Baby sets down the tray.

"You have a lovely home," Carmen says, grinning stupidly.

"Thank you."

"I brought pictures of my trip to Japan," she says. "If you're interested."

"Course I'm interested," Baby says. "Miguel is my brother, too." She tries to sound genuine, but the truth is, she doesn't remember him. How could she? She was two years old when he and their father left the camp. She doesn't remember her father either.

"They're in my suitcase," Carmen says, standing. Baby points down the hall to the guest room. "Be right back," Carmen says, leaving.

Isabel pats the vacant space beside her and Baby sits. "I missed you," Baby says, and she means it. Isabel bumps her shoulder into her little sister's. "Me, too. I'm sorry I couldn't make it for Christmas."

"I know." Baby hands her sister a tumbler of tea. "Carmen hates me."

Isabel takes a sip. "She doesn't hate you. She's just angry about this whole reparations thing and I guess she's taking it out on you."

"It's not my fault," she says, jabbing a knife in the cheese to carve out a healthy chunk.

"I know. She was just so disappointed in the outcome of the lawsuit. We all are. I mean, you all got $20,000 and the rest of us only get $5000. It just doesn't seem fair."

"It's not," Baby says, trying to sound like a disinterested party.

"Here they are!" Carmen says, shuffling in with a Wal-Mart shopping bag. She reaches in to pull out a fat envelope and squeezes between the two sisters, sliding out photos, passing them right and left. "Here's a shot from the plane," Carmen says. "And this is the airport. The baggage claim area."

Baby nods and smiles and occasionally grunts, but she's wondering if she should put the Jell-O mold back in the refrigerator, and if the mail has come. She looks out the front window for the mail truck. No. It's not there.

"Here is Miguel," Carmen says. "He has Mami's eyes, see?"

Baby squints at the picture: A stooped, old man next to a speckled dog. Both looking malnourished. It's hard to believe this is her brother. He sent her a photo once, of himself and his wife in front of the Hiroshima memorial. He wrote her a long letter, seven pages, in Spanish. She had to have her dental hygienist translate it, having long since forgotten the Spanish she spoke as a child in the camp. She wrote him back in English, but he never replied. She thinks of him, from time to time, when the Weather Channel reports on typhoons in Japan, or earthquakes, or volcano activity. She offers a prayer for his safety, and his wife's, and the niece and two nephews she has never met.

"Here's Papi's grave," Carmen says. And there it is. A patch of grass inlaid with a tiny rectangular stone that reads: Born Lima, Peru 1900; Died Nagasaki, Japan 1945. Baby tries to muster some sadness, grief, but it just won't come, even as she hears her sisters' sniffles, sees the wetness in their eyes, on their cheeks. Then her eyes are moist, too. Not for Papi, for herself. At least Carmen and Isabel had him for awhile. They have memories. She has nothing.

"What were they like?" Baby asks.

"What?" Isabel says.

"Mami and Papi." These words feel strange in her mouth. Foreign.

They don't roll off her tongue the way Mama and Daddy Adkins so naturally do.

Carmen and Isabel look at each other, then at their little sister. Carmen's shoulders go down and she pats Baby's knee. "Mami was like a bird," she says. "Singing all day. Made up songs about butterflies and frogs—"

"And stars that played hooky," Isabel says.

"¡Aí, sí!" Carmen says, laughing.

"She would have loved you," Isabel says.

"She would have pinched your chubby cheeks," Carmen adds. "You were such a fat baby. Gordita."

"Papi made sure of that," Isabel says. "All our camp milk rations went into your bottle."

"That's why I have such bad teeth," Carmen says, tapping a gray incisor.

Baby frowns.

Carmen squeezes Baby's knee. "I'm just kidding. You kept Papi alive after Mami died. You have her nose."

"And her smile," Isabel adds.

"Sí. Papi doted on you. Showed you off to all the other internees. Oh the fuss they made over you."

"Even the Germans and Italians thought you were a beautiful baby," Isabel says. "Schönes mädchen, they said. Bambina bella!"

"It's no wonder Cowboy Bob wanted you," Carmen says.

Baby is cowed. This is the first true compliment she has received from Carmen. She looks at her sister, but Carmen's eyes are downcast, glazed over as if she is miles away. Or years.

"But we wanted you, too," she whispers. "After they traded Papi and Miguel for American soldiers, we wanted you all for ourselves. Algo bonito all for ourselves."

"Hush," Isabel whispers. "No use reliving it. And besides. We have her now. Right here."

Carmen lifts her head and surprises them all when she chucks her finger under Baby's chin. "Sí," she says. "Ahora, sí." She looks deep into Baby's eyes searching for something, desperate to find something. Baby is afraid she won't find it, or maybe she will, so she looks away fast.

"Shall I give her our present?" Carmen says.

Isabel nods.

Carmen reaches in the Wal-Mart bag and pulls out a fat package wrapped in red paper. "Feliz cumpleaños," she says.

"Happy birthday," Isabel says.

Baby unwraps the gift: a photo album with a leather tongue and brass latch to keep it closed. Baby clicks the latch, flips the cover, and sees a crinkled photo of a middle aged man posing stoically in traditional Japanese garb. Dark hair slicked back. Thick mustache covering his upper lip. The inscription reads: *Grandpa Takei, 1899*.

Isabel says, "That was taken right before he and Grandma moved to Peru."

"Where's Grandma?" Baby asks, more interested in her outfit than her image.

Carmen shrugs. "Camera shy, I guess, but imagine a couple their age starting over like that."

"Papi said it was because of the Meiji Restoration," Isabel says. "Everything becoming modern and Westernized. All those growing pains. He said it was a difficult time for farmers, for everyone, really."

This all sounds vaguely familiar to Baby, like something she saw on the History Channel, not a tale passed down from her kin.

Baby turns the page and sucks in her breath: a photo of her mother and father on their wedding day. Both standing so stiff in their fine cloths, father's chest puffed up, right hand slipped into his vest. Mother's hair piled high on her head, held in place by an elaborate comb. She holds an unfolded fan to her chest. Baby has never seen her image before. All the family history was lost back in Peru: photos, birth certificates, snippets of hair. Or so Baby thought. Her eyes cloud as she touches the face that looks so much like hers. The crooked smile. Head cocked to the side.

She flips the page and there she is again, her mother, standing on a vast veranda crowded with plants, an infant in her arms.

"That's Miguel," Carmen says. "And the house where we were born."

"All except you," Isabel adds, an apology.

In the next one her father stands on a tree stump, a young boy at his side, maybe seven or eight. Miguel, no doubt. They are surrounded by workers, their hats in their hands, some holding bandsaws and scythes.

"Papi's rubber plantation," Isabel says. "I used to love to run through the trees with my arms outstretched."

"And hide for hours so you wouldn't have to do your chores," Carmen scolds.

"Especially during a storm when you could stay dry under those enormous leaves and listen to thunder cracking overhead, roaring rain."

"And Mami and me making supper in the kitchen wondering where you were."

Baby sifts through photo after photo: the plantation; Mami and Papi with Miguel; then Carmen; then Isabel. All looking so content.

In the last photo Papi and Miguel sit in claw-footed chairs. Isabel and Carmen sit on low stools beside them. Mami stands behind her husband. Carmen taps her fingernail on Mami's face. "You know why she is behind this chair?"

"Why?" Baby says.

"To hide her bulging stomach. She was four months pregnant with you."

"Ah!" Isabel says. "So this really is the whole family."

"No," Baby whispers, wanting to move that chair to see, to believe that she was ever a part of this family, this culture that is as foreign to her as Japan must have been to her father and brother when they were sent there.

"Sí," Carmen says. "Together for such a brief time."

Amazed, Baby stares at the picture trying desperately to accept that this is her family, her blood. But this photo belongs in another era, another country, another family's scrapbook.

"Where did you get these?" is all she can say.

Carmen sighs deeply. "The night they came for us, one of the workers—"

"Felix Rios," Isabel says.

"Sí. Felix snuck in and grabbed these from the walls."

"Not a minute too soon, either. Officials soon returned to steal everything they could find."

Baby's mind fills with flitting sepia images of soldiers rifling through her family's jewelry boxes and china cabinets and toy chests in the middle of the night.

"I bet the townspeople helped themselves, too," Carmen says. "They hated us even before the war. *¡Salir Nips!*" she says. "I remember The Night of Plundering. So many Japanese businesses and homes destroyed." Her eyes harden at a memory Baby doesn't dare ask to be shared.

"Not everyone felt that way. Some were our good friends," Isabel says.

"Pah," Carmen says. "Friends who wouldn't let us back in our own country after the war. *Good riddance*," she says. "They probably danced on the pier when our boats sailed."

Suddenly Baby is immersed in her own memory, just a snippet that she buried long ago under piles of fan letters and interview requests and autograph signings. She and Cowboy Bob riding in a black convertible, waving at bystanders during a Christmas parade. Or was it Easter? Baby isn't sure, but she is absolutely certain about the gang of men who rushed the car yelling: *Zipperhead go home!* Throwing something, not rocks, but eggs, at the car, at her, until local police chased the men away.

"Look how long Felix looked for us just to return these," Isabel adds, patting the album.

Carmen purses her lips, but Baby is trying to understand her thunking heart. She puts a hand to her chest. "People loved me," she whispers, conjuring images of bright-faced studio audiences, their hearty applause, the Lucky Baby look-alike contests. She takes all of that, heaps it on the bad memory, and tamps it down hard.

The doorbell rings and Baby is jolted back to the present, to her squat house on a cul-de-sac in Tormenta Falls, Texas.

"I'll get it!" Joe calls from the kitchen. He bursts out, Kiss the Cook apron dangling from his neck. Joe opens the door and in walks a nearly six-foot blonde in a tangerine dress.

Baby slams the photo album closed and plops it on the coffee table. "Linda!" she wails, jumping straight out of her seat to rush to her guest. Baby's arms circle the woman whose hands are loaded with yellow roses and a bundle of multicolored envelopes and a shoebox-sized package wrapped in brown paper.

"Happy birthday!" Linda says, kissing Baby on both cheeks. "I ran into your mailman."

Joe takes the flowers and the cards and starts flipping through them. He holds out an aqua envelope. "Hurricane, West Virginia! That's a first."

Baby grabs the box, frantically scanning for the sender's name. "It's from Cowboy Bob," she says solemnly.

Joe leans over to verify. "Really? What is it?"

"How should I know?" Baby says, giving the box a gentle shake, wondering what he could have possibly sent. Something grand, she is sure: a cut crystal vase, a hand carved statue, an emerald necklace and earrings to make up for all the ties and cotton handkerchiefs she's been faithfully sending though she's never gotten one thing. He's very busy, after all.

"Open it and see!" Joe says.

Baby looks at the box in her hands containing who-knows-what, but it's better than any birthday or Christmas present she's ever anticipated and she wants to prolong it. "After supper," Baby says. She sets the box firmly on top of the photo album and gives it a pat.

Baby aims Linda at her sisters. "You remember Isabel."

Linda reaches forward and shakes Isabel's hand, silver bangles around Linda's wrist clinking. "Of course. Good to see you again."

"And this is Carmen," Baby says.

Linda leans forward, arm outstretched, fingers ready to grip, but Carmen hasn't taken her eyes from her family album practically hidden beneath Bob's gift. "Mucho gusto," she mumbles without looking up.

Linda withdraws her ignored hand. "Pleasure to meet you, too."

The phone rings and Joe bounds to the kitchen to answer.

"It's like Grand Central today!" Baby says, pleased.

"Looks like you got a good husband," Carmen says. "He dotes on you."

"This is nothing," Isabel says. "Wait till you see how he tucks her in bed."

"He does not."

"He does!" Linda says. "I've been through three husbands and not one treated me the way Joe treats Baby. She's a regular princess."

Baby blushes, but she can't deny that Joe pampers her. He cooks her favorite dishes and scrubs the kitchen floors and keeps track of the finances. No wonder Carmen is sad, Baby thinks, and Isabel, too, to some extent. Neither ever married, though Baby imagines Isabel must have had suitors. Such a pretty girl, once. Of course they didn't have Baby's advantages. No Baptist couple ever took them in, accepted them as daughters. Willed them their houses and late-model Fords and modest inheritances. No, they had none of that.

Joe bolts from the kitchen. "That was Channel 7!" he says, twisting his apron. "They want to tape a segment about you for the 10:00 o'clock news!"

"When!" Baby asks.

"Hour or so," Joe says.

Baby's hands go to her face, her hair, her shirt. "What should I wear?"

Joe looks her up and down, considering. "The red blouse and black skirt."

Baby nods. "Yes," she says. "What earrings?"

"The pearls!" Joe says, as if she should have known that.

"We better get you dolled up," Linda says.

She and Baby are ready to bolt but Joe blurts: "We should eat first. You can change after."

"Good idea," Baby says. "Wouldn't want to be on TV with barbeque sauce on my shirt."

"Or your teeth," Linda says, following Baby and Joe to the dining room. "Have you been using that whitener I gave you?"

Isabel and Carmen look at each other and decide they're supposed to get up and go eat, too.

Baby and Linda cackle and chatter and haul dish after dish to the table. Joe brings in the brisket and slices it up, doling out hefty slabs. Carmen and Isabel sit side by side, poking their forks at the pounds of meat Joe piled onto their plates, red juices pooling around globs of mashed potatoes and deviled eggs. They aren't used to Texas portions and Carmen says, "Ungh."

"What?" Joe says, expecting at least a *yum*.

Carmen's face contorts into a look of disgust. "I'll never be able to eat all this."

Baby pulls in her chair at the head of the table. "We don't skimp around here."

Carmen looks at Baby's gut and opens her mouth, but Isabel cuts in: "It's delicious."

"Thank you," Joe says, mouth full of potatoes.

Linda jabbers away about what eye shadow Baby should use, what foundation, lipstick.

Baby listens to her and the clank of bangle bracelets and silverware, ice cubes settling, Joe's jaw happily popping, but she can't help peeking over her sisters' shoulders for a glimpse of Bob's gift waiting so prominently, so expectantly, on her coffee table. It could hold anything. But what's most important is who it's from. Finally, a gift from Cowboy Bob.

"Baby and I met in high school," Linda says to Carmen.

"That's nice," Carmen says, returning half of her meat to the serving platter.

"That's right," Joe says, ignoring the slight. "You should see the yearbook pictures. Same hairdo, same sweater set."

"Everyone called us the Bobbsey twins," Linda says.

Carmen and Isabel look from Baby to Linda.

"We were in the pep squad together," Linda says. "And the drama club."

Carmen's face draws up like a wrinkled fig as Linda goes on and on about their sleepovers, about rolling each other's hair, about stuffing their bras with their fathers' socks. The hours they spent in front of the bathroom mirror primping and tweezing and popping pimples.

Carmen listens intently, but with each new story her foot taps faster until she's thrumming a frantic drum roll under the table.

"And don't forget the school talent shows!" Linda says, waving a forked shrimp at Carmen and Isabel. "Every year for the grand finale Baby came on stage in a little girl dress—course it was cut bigger, just made to look all frilly and poufy—and she'd climb on top of the piano and belt out 'The Yellow Rose of Texas' or 'God Bless America' and I swear there wasn't a dry eye in the gym."

"I bet you had the boyfriends lined up, too," Joe says. "I know I would have been waiting at that stage door with a handful of posies."

Baby looks at the chandelier over the table, the pretty way the light reflects in the glass droplets.

"Those dumb boys at our school were too intimidated by such a big star," Linda says. "They couldn't even work up the courage to ask her to the prom."

Carmen looks at Isabel, then Baby, whose lips are pursed into a tight magenta rose.

"I bet they're kicking theirselves to this very day," Joe says. "Could have had a date with a great big star."

"That's right," Linda says. "Bunch of dopes. But Baby showed all of them, didn't you. You married the best boy of all."

Baby looks at her husband, sitting there adoring her. He is so proud of her fame, and patient about her celebrity, always happy to let fans come up and say hello. Baby looks over at Linda, another woman at the table without a husband, and feels a knot of guilt behind her left eye. "High school was fun," Baby admits. "Some of the best times of my life."

Carmen snorts and crosses her arms over her chest.

Linda ignores her and says, "It was a wonderful time. Pity we can't all stay back there."

Carmen sucks a sliver of meat between her teeth. "Isabel and I went to high school in the camp. We wore uniforms and the five of us lived in a room even smaller than this."

"Carmen," Isabel says.

"We had a yearbook, too," Carmen says. "And a band. And a swimming pool. Crystal City was a model camp. Weren't we lucky?"

"Stop it," Isabel says.

"What!" She juts her chin at Linda and Baby. "They have no idea."

"This isn't the time," Isabel says.

"When *is* the time, Isabel. We are old women, now, and Baby— Rosa," she looks at Baby. "Your name is *Rosa*—acts like she does not remember. How can you not remember, Rosa, the nights you shivered under those scratchy blankets, or stood in line at the latrine. Have you forgotten our games? Find the pebble. How long can it take you to eat?"

Baby sets down her knife and fork and looks at the butter dish. "It was so long ago, another life."

Carmen looks around Baby's dining room: the hutch filled with china; tidy pictures of birds and fruit hung symmetrically on the walls; photos of her foster parents, and Cowboy Bob, and Baby in a white wedding dress beside Joe in a sky blue tux.

"Yes," Carmen says. "You've had a different life than us. That's for sure."

"I remember a squirrel," Baby says.

"What's that?" Carmen says.

Baby pleats the hem of the tablecloth and tries to untangle this fuzzy knot. "I remember peeking through the floorboards at piles of dirt. And there was a squirrel—"

"It was a rat," Carmen says. "We called him el ladrón because he snuck in at night and stole hunks of bread and dug holes in the rice."

"We thought he was a prisoner, too," Isabel says. "So we didn't have the heart to set a trap."

"There was a lady," Baby says. "With white hair in a bun. She slapped my hands with a stick when I cried."

"Señora Ito," Isabel says. "She was a widow they put in with us after they traded her son away. What a grouch. Wouldn't let us talk after 7:00 p.m. even when we were doing homework."

"She farted all night and blamed it on el ladrón," Carmen says. "As if a tiny rodent could make so much noise. Or smell!" Carmen emits a throaty cackle that makes her head shake, her earrings jangle, and Baby realizes she has never heard her sister really laugh.

Baby says: "You took good care of me, didn't you?"

"We tried out best," Carmen says. "But we were just children ourselves."

Linda sniffs loudly and everyone turns to see mascara trickling down her cheeks. "What they did to you all was atrocious," she says. "I mean, Japanese Americans had it bad enough, but they yanked you all from your country and then called you illegal aliens so you weren't entitled to the $20,000, which, by the way, wasn't much in the first place. I told Baby, I was glad the JLAs brought their own lawsuit, but this settlement is pathetic. I wouldn't take that piddly $5000. I'd hire my own attorney and go in with both barrels cocked."

Carmen looks at Isabel, then Baby, then Joe. "It takes money to hire a lawyer."

Isabel grips Carmen's wrist. "Later."

Carmen nods toward Linda. "She brought it up. And I just need a thousand dollars for the retainer," Carmen says, hands out, palms up.

Baby looks at her husband and now she knows why Carmen has come all this way to see her.

Joe clears his throat. "Thousand dollars is a lot of money."

"Not to you," Carmen says. "Baby must have something left from that $20—"

"That was twelve years ago," Joe says, shaking his head. "We really don't."

"Of course," Carmen says, head slumping forward as if every vertebra in her spine suddenly melted.

Baby looks at her sister, face so tired and worn. Carmen hasn't had an easy life and what does she have to look forward to? No husband. No mailbox filled with birthday cards from adoring fans. No wall full of glorious memories that no one can take away. No ten o'clock news coming for an interview. No present from Cowboy Bob just waiting to be opened. A feeling swells in Baby's chest and she says: "We'll give you our check when it comes."

"Shut up," Joe says.

Carmen's head perks up. "What check?"

Joe stands, napkin tucked in his shirt. "I said shut up, Baby."

"But she needs it more than we do," Baby says. "She could hire a good lawyer with that $5000."

"What $5000?" Isabel says.

"You know," Baby says. "The JLA settlement."

"Oh no," Joe says, shrinking back to his seat just as Isabel stands, a fork in her hand. Her mouth opens and closes and opens again and she stares first at Joe, then Baby.

"What?" Baby says, stunned by this lack of gratitude for her generosity. Isabel stares at her with a face full of something Baby has never seen before.

"That money is not for you," Isabel seethes.

Baby is dumbfounded. "Of course it is," she says, looking at Joe for help. He offers none. "We got the paperwork just like you did," she says. "With a postage paid return envelope."

Isabel pounds her fork against the table, rattling glasses, making Baby flinch. "It was a mistake. There's barely enough in the fund to pay legitimate claims and you, who already got three times as much and wasted it on a ridiculous hot tub and sauna—"

"I thought you liked the hot tub," Baby says, hurt. She might expect this from Carmen, but never Isabel.

"You stupid brat!" Isabel says. "You think you deserve everything, but you're not entitled to this."

"But I'm giving it to you!" Baby says, absolutely flabbergasted.

"It's not yours to give! Don't you understand?"

Baby's face is a blank china plate.

Carmen pats Isabel's hand. "I don't think she does. Do you, Baby?"

Baby shakes her head slowly from side to side. "Joe takes care of all that."

All heads turn toward Joe, who tugs the napkin from his collar and tosses it on the floor. "This is none of your business," he says to the sisters.

Isabel faces him. "It's none of *your* business, you sneaky con—"

"That's enough!" Carmen says.

Joe slowly rises. "Whatever I do is for Baby," he says. His ears redden as he looks at his bride and his voice cracks when he says, "It's all for you." Joe turns his back on them and starts for the kitchen. Before he gets there he pauses and says: "Don't forget the pearl earrings, Baby. They make your face shine." Baby watches Joe leave and something leaves with him, some inexplicable thing that makes the room appear smaller, the drapes appear dated, carpet worn, wallpaper dingy. A sudden rumble that sounds very much like Joe's '56 Corvette, a squeal of tires down the back alley.

A fruit fly skitters from one dish to the next as Baby looks toward the kitchen willing Joe to come back, *come back*. She feels her sisters' eyes on her but she wants out from under their scrutiny, wants to run from them and this feeling, this dread that's bubbling up inside her, rattling the steel celebrity framework that has undergirded her whole marriage, her life.

Linda stops wringing her napkin and stands. "The meal was delicious, Baby."

Baby looks up at her friend, hears the disconnected words streaming from her mouth.

"I'll call you tomorrow," Linda whispers. She tiptoes past them and all three sisters hear the front door quietly close.

Isabel, still standing, looks down on Baby.

Carmen clears her throat. "You better go change for your interview," she says.

"What?" Baby says.

"The newspeople," Carmen says.

"Oh. Yes." Baby rises and plunks her knife and fork in her tea glass then reaches for Joe's silverware, too.

"Isabel and I will clear the table," Carmen says. "You go change and then we'll have some birthday cake."

"Cake," Baby says. "I should have offered Linda cake."

Carmen stands and moves beside Baby. She grips her by the shoulders and urges her toward the hall. "And then you can open your present from Cowboy Bob."

"The present," Baby says. A dim light flickers somewhere deep inside her. She looks at the fat package on the table that just might contain a salve, or glue strong enough to restore whatever this is that's falling apart.

In her room, Baby closes the door and stands before her closet jammed with flowery dresses and lacy blouses on quilted hangers. On the shelf, a tidy row of shiny, black pumps, stacks of round straw hats with flowing ribbons. Her sisters argue in the kitchen; their harsh words tumble down the hall and squeeze under Baby's door. Something about Joe, his intentions, his real reason for marrying Baby.

It's ridiculous, Baby thinks, going to the dresser to pull out Joe's junk drawer where he keeps his good watch and his checkbook and the spare keys to the Corvette. There are also stacks and stacks of papers. Baby watches fingers unfolding sheet after sheet, not her fingers, opening them to read, trying to make sense of bank statements with columns that add up to sizable sums. And there are the JLA forms and she remembers the day Joe said: *Just sign right there. I'll fill them out later.* She finds a Xeroxed copy of the form he sent in. She scans it and stops half way down, staring at the words, the incorrect words. Baby reads the line over and over until it becomes a kind of mantra. *Born: Lima, Peru. Born: Lima, Peru.* And because she has to she formulates the question: What's so wrong about that? So what if Joe put in the wrong place of her birth? She was conceived in Peru and would have, should have been born in the same house as Miguel and Carmen and Isabel. What's $5000 to pay for that loss? What's $20,000? Her family would still be together if not for the Americans, the stupid Americans! Then she remembers Cowboy Bob. And her adoring Texas fans. And of course Joe. Red-blooded Joe. Baby's head feels woozy, legs rubbery, and she slumps onto the same bed where Joan and Wally Adkins slept for 53 years.

Half an hour later Baby scuffs down the hall in her skirt and blouse. She grips her shoes in one hand and fiddles with her right pearl earring with the other.

Carmen gazes out the front window at the sun sliding behind trees. From the west, a gray wall of clouds rolls in, smoky wisps twirling out from underneath. She looks up when Baby enters. "You look like a movie star."

"Thank you," Baby says, sitting on the couch to slip on her shoes.

A toilet flushes and Isabel comes down the hall, too. She can't look at Baby, but she sits in the wingback chair across from her, Cowboy Bob's gift and their family photo album between them, brass buckle gleaming.

Carmen goes into the kitchen and Isabel and Baby listen to cabinets and drawers being opened. Minor cussing. Moments later Carmen pads in, Baby's red velvet cake in her hands. Twenty lit candles flickering. Carmen clears her throat and starts warbling, "Happy birthday to you. Happy birthday to you." She looks at Isabel, urging her to join in, finally nudging her foot so she will, which she does, but in a woeful voice that sounds like howling wind.

When they finish the song Carmen holds the cake in front of Baby's face.

"Make a wish," Carmen says.

Baby closes her eyes, and sitting there, face illuminated by the kind candle light, Baby looks like a child, ready to wish for a bike or a Barbie. She's wishing for much more than that. Finally she opens her eyes and blows out all twenty candles in one breath.

"You get your wish," Isabel says.

Carmen starts to cut thin slivers of cake, but looks at Baby and decides on fat wedges.

Baby forgets about the ice cream in the freezer, just shovels in one forkful after another, barely chewing or even tasting the cream cheese frosting she especially loves.

"The brisket was delicious," Isabel says. "Joe is a good cook."

Baby looks up to see if her sister is joking, egging her on, but she doesn't appear to be.

Carmen's head bobs in agreement. "He certainly was a good catch."

"He was, wasn't he," Baby says, feeling buoyed. "He bought me these earrings, you know," she says, touching one of the pearls. "Only someone who truly loves you would buy you real pearls."

"That's right," Carmen says. "Isn't it, Isabel."

Isabel looks at Baby, face practically pleading. "Yes," she says. "He must love you a great deal."

Movement from the front window and Baby looks out at the crepe myrtle in her front yard frantically swaying.

"It's going to storm!" Baby says, jumping up to open the front door. A gust of cool air blasts in, whipping her hair, her skirt. "Finally, an end to this heat!" she says, forcing the door closed. "Now Joe will be back any minute!"

Carmen and Isabel look at her, puzzled.

"He doesn't like to drive his Corvette in the rain," Baby says.

"Oh," the sisters say, but their eyebrows remain furrowed.

Carmen points to the brown package. "Time to open your gift."

"Yes!" Baby says, plopping on the couch, pulling the package to her knees. She rips off the brown paper and is disheartened to see that the box inside is not wrapped in festive birthday paper. It's just a tattered shoe box, yellow envelope taped to the lid. Baby slides out the note. It's from Cowboy Bob's secretary, not Cowboy Bob. As Baby reads it aloud she tries not to draw conclusions about the similarity between the secretary's handwriting and Bob's signature on her birthday and Christmas cards all these years.

Enclosed are the last of Cowboy Bob's papers re: The Cowboy Bob Show. Bob has gone downhill quite a bit this past year and I know he would want you to have these.

The cake in Baby's belly churns. No crystal vase, no carved statue, no jewelry. Baby is glad Joe isn't here to see this. He would be sorely disappointed, too.

Baby lifts the cover and a musty smell wafts out. She tugs out wads of aged envelopes and passes some to Isabel and Carmen. The sisters sit unfolding fragile letters, most addressed to Cowboy Bob care of WTBC, the station that produced and broadcasted the show. Inside are requests for autographed pictures. Heart-shaped cards with real lipstick kisses. A few mothers enclosed photos of eligible daughters. There are internal memos about scheduled guests: dogs who play ping pong, chickens who type. Some date to even before Baby was a cast member. There's a letter from Sheldon Rosenberg, the executive producer, congratulating Bob on his continued success, his devoted audience.

Baby remembers Mr. Rosenberg. Always so tidy in his pinstriped suit and wingtip shoes. A fresh carnation in his lapel every morning. Kept his jacket pockets filled with suckers and Necco Wafers just for Baby.

"This one is about me!" Baby says, holding up a sheet of onion skin. It's dated June 7, 1946. Mr. Rosenberg informs Cowboy Bob they will be adding a new cast member. A little girl from Crystal City to help start the healing process. *Rosa Takei,* the letter reads. *What a lucky baby.*

"This is how it all started," Carmen says. "Imagine if he never had the idea?"

Baby cannot imagine. She refuses to imagine and it's silly to even try.

Baby unfolds the next letter, also from Sheldon to Cowboy Bob: *I'm disheartened by your resistance—*

Baby stops. She looks at the paper in her hand. The words on the page that are increasingly difficult to read because they are shaking, vowels and consonants banging against each other.

"What?" Carmen says.

"Nothing," Baby says, trying to laugh. Trying to tuck the paper back in the envelope before it is too late. And where is Joe? Why isn't he here to share in this wonderful gift sent all the way from Florida by Cowboy Bob?

The paper won't fit, and it won't fit, so Isabel takes it from Baby's hands. "What is it?" she says, unfolding it to read aloud:

I'm disheartened by your resistance, but my decision is final. Your racist comments about this child are appalling. Be advised: they will not be tolerated on the set. This is not up for debate, Bob. The girl stays. If you cannot work with her in a professional manner, then I will expect your resignation forthwith.

Baby sits too still on the couch, tightly gripping the shoe box as she tries to make sense of the letter. It's a forgery, of course. A cruel trick Bob is playing. Tossing it in with the others to make a joke at her expense.

"Bob always had a strange sense of humor," Baby says. But suddenly she is back in that black convertible during the Easter parade, men throwing raw eggs, calling her names, screaming at her to go home. *Go Home!* How she wanted to press her tiny body against Cowboy Bob's side, have him drape his arm around her to protect. To keep her safe. But when she scooted toward him, even as an egg splattered on his fringed leather jacket, he shoved her away, eyes full of loathing, mouth pressed into a self-righteous smirk.

Baby sets the box clumsily on top of the photo album, but it tips over and falls to the floor, spilling letters and post cards that might reveal more horrible truths Baby cannot bear. She numbly stands and walks to the picture window to look out at black clouds swirling in.

"It's going to storm," she says again. "Joe will be back soon. He doesn't drive his Corvette in the rain."

"We know," Isabel says.

"It's getting dark," Baby says about the storm, about the room. She should turn on a light, but she doesn't. It would make something real. Some hideous thing she can ignore as long as it is dark. She sees her sisters' reflections behind her, the pathetic way they look at her. Ha! Them feeling sorry for her. If Joe were here he would laugh at Bob's joke. He would understand this joke, however cruel. And with the lights out she can better watch for his headlights. Surely he will be home soon. Any minute now Joe will pull up and she'll run to him and he'll hug her and pat her hair and tell her everything will be all right. What a good laugh they will all have.

Then there are headlights, heading for her, and she can breathe again as they pull into her driveway.

"He's home!" Baby says.

Walls collapse in her chest when she realize it isn't Joe at all, but Channel 7 coming to interview her, to invariably ask what it was like to work with Cowboy Bob all those years. And what is she to say? *Wonderful. He was like a father to me.* Her standard answer for the last fifty-four years. A man gets out of the van and opens the trunk. He looks at the sky, the impending rain, and wraps something in plastic, the camera, no doubt. A woman gets out, too. Baby recognizes her face, sees the microphone in her hand and Baby steps back from the window. If she slips deep enough into shadows maybe they won't see her, maybe they'll think she isn't home. That she forgot. And perhaps they'll forget Baby, too.

A knock at the door and Isabel and Carmen both stand. "I'll get it," Carmen says.

"No," Baby whispers, holding her arm out as a gate to keep her sisters from nearing the door.

The three awkwardly stand, listening to the persistent knocking. Harder and harder.

Isabel says, "I'll tell them to go away."

"No!" Baby says, looking out the window, straining to see into the distance. "Just wait."

"For what?" Isabel says.

"For Joe," Baby says. "He'll tell me what to say."

Baby can feel her sisters' stares, but she doesn't care as she looks outside at the crepe myrtle whipping in the wind, practically horizontal. Crimson buds holding on for dear life. Now rain pelting the glass, wet streaks blurring her vision. And the news crew banging on the door, yelling for her: "Lucky Baby! Are you in there? It's Channel 7!"

Baby stands firmly and doesn't breathe as she hears the storm beating down, fists battering the door, her sisters imploring: "Baby, let them in! Just let them in!" Baby ignores them all because she knows that Joe will be here any minute, any second now to tell her what to say. How to act. She stares out the window without blinking, praying, willing her husband to appear, begging Joe to appear.

A crack of lightning and the room bursts with light, then is thrown back into blackness, except for the glint on the photo album's brass latch. A voice in Rosa's head begins calling, begging, not her own voice, exactly, but one that sounds very much like Carmen, or Isabel, pleading for Joe, or for someone, for some dear one, to come home.

The Wife You Wanted

I hover in the foyer for five minutes, my heels digging little graves in the plush carpet as I pace back and forth, back and forth before the muted wall mural: cypress trees and tranquil streams meant to console. They don't soothe me because I know you're in there, Tommy, waiting. And the thought of you, the image, even after all these years, makes my fingers tremble. Finally I clench my teeth and rush into the teeming room, though I'm knocked back a step by the nauseating sweetness of too many flowers. I push through it, looking frenetically for familiar faces, peering into sagging jowls and sun-creased eyes, trying to subtract twenty-five years. Do I know you? Did I know you?

Across the room your mother stands like the grande dame she is, only ever bowing down to one person: you. Polishing your shoes, bringing your hot lunch to school every day because she knew the few foods you would eat: lemon-pepper chicken livers your favorite, yikes, and for a minute of my life I thought I would have to learn how to make them, if not eat them. (Rest assured. The ironic snobbery is not lost on me, who lapped up pâté in the '80s when I lived in Dallas—or was it Seattle?—this exquisite cuisine that couldn't possibly be kin to the common chicken livers served up back in West Virginia.)

I walk toward her, this tiny woman—a foot shorter than me—with a monolithic presence, who scrutinizes me so completely I want to run back to the foyer. But her mouth opens and out pours my name in one long, cave-buried howl: "Julie?"

"Yes," I assure her.

She swoops in for an urgent embrace that nearly cracks my spine. "You came all the way from Chicago?"

"Yes," I lie, because I can't tell her that I was in town visiting my mother anyway, that it's a monumental coincidence.

"Come," she says, strapping one arm around my waist to guide me through the crowd, well-wishers patting her shoulder, kissing her cheek as we pass. We could be at a tea party, your stoic mother and I, the way she nods and smiles, the lilt in her step as she ushers me to your father, slumped in a chair, staggered. Clearly this is no tea party for him.

"You remember our Julie," Frances says.

Our Julie.

Your father raises his handsome head—I always thought he was handsome, tall, chiseled, so different from his scrawny son. Cute, yes, but you cannot deny the scrawny.

"Julie?" he repeats, a fleeting zap of current in his vacant eyes.

He stands and I cup his cold hand in mine.

"Have you seen him yet?" he says.

My heart dives into my stomach. "No."

Frances grips my hand. "I'll take you. He's right over here."

Your father collapses back into his chair as your mother whisks me away.

"This is Julie," she chirrups to people, relatives, who may or may not have heard of me. Introducing me as if I were her daughter-in-law. "She's a columnist, you know." As if I deserve a place of honor and respect on this unhinging day.

"That's Julie," someone whispers as I pass.

The crowd around you parts as Frances approaches; they understand protocol.

I suck in my breath before taking you in.

And there you are.

Your mother says: "Isn't he handsome?"

I have to say yes, and you do look pleased, that pre-formed smile at this reunion.

But the truth is, Tommy, you also look like a used car salesman with your hair slicked back. Striated comb streaks plowed through whatever pomade they used to tame that wild hair I remember so well, wispy. All Peter Frampton, tips tinged gold by the sun. You're not golden now, though you're still as wiry as Frampton. Nose still elfin. High forehead only etched with a few well-earned wrinkles. Under that suit coat your folded arms cratered with cigarette burns from all those games of chicken you bragged about, reminding me of your rough roots: you West End, redneck, grease-monkey boy with your GTO that grumbled through my hilly East End neighborhood night after night. My stodgy fundamentalist neighbors tisk-tisking from behind pulled curtains: *Get a muffler!* They didn't understand about hot rods and shag-carpeted dashboards.

Neither did I until you started driving me home from school the spring of our senior year. Your West End, soon-to-be-ex-girlfriend's picture taped over your 8-track tape player. Looking not *un*like me— or any other '70s girl: long auburn hair parted in the middle, straightened by chemicals or irons or orange juice can curlers because there was really no other acceptable style back then for the cool. Before taking me home you parked under the accordion awning at Dwight's and cranked down your window, pressed the button that would summon the crackling voice: "What'll it be?"

Two Cokes and a large fries.

Always.

It felt as if we were diving back into the '50s when the carhop brought our tray. We nestled our weeping drinks between our legs—no built-in cup holders yet—the condensation dampening our thighs. We dunked our fries in ketchup and talked about . . . what? School? Doubtful, since both of us were more interested in getting stoned in the alley than required reading: Thomas Hardy and Willa Cather. Blah. My leaning back then was Carlos Castaneda and Kahlil Gibran, mind-altering writers for mind-altering years. Your obsession was car engines, and you spouted soliloquies about carburetors and fuel pumps in another language. You could have been conjugating Latin verbs.

Perhaps we talked about life after graduation. Your father buying you a NAPA Auto Parts franchise in Kermit or Pinch. I can't recall exactly, though I remember that it was miles from anything remotely resembling civilization—whatever that meant to me at the time. Certainly there were no institutions of higher learning. But this was your father's grand idea that would set you for life, or so you claimed. You crowed about take-home pay that sounded like riches, your intention exactly.

Today, with your mother beside me, I look at your hands, your fingernails, for greasy residue, the mechanic's tattoos, and there they are, still, because no amount of Gunk hand cleaner could unloose them then, or now.

Then I hop back into the GTO and scooch up beside you, Steve Miller or Bob Seger spilling from the radio as we discussed my future: college, because I knew I needed a skill. Learned that lesson by working at another drive-in hot dog stand and watching those fifty- and sixty-year-old women slap patties onto the grill, concoct the secret sauce, boil thousands of hot dogs day after day after day, their feet swelling, the sweat pouring in that 114° kitchen, earning slightly more than minimum wage. The sole bread winners because of their disabled husbands, and now they were raising their grandkids, too. I stood beside them rolling up hot dogs, refilling the bun steamers, the seared burns on my arms and legs—the short order's tattoos— worth the meager paycheck spent not on a husband's medications or a granddaughter's Dairy Queen birthday cake, but on pot and mescaline and beer. (I confess that I hide this mustard- and onion-soaked chapter from my NPR-supporting, peach-martini-sipping neighbors in the Chicago burbs.)

The lives of those beehived, hamburger-flipping women were as foreign to me as yours, living as you did *way* out in Spring Valley: ten miles from town that might as well have been a million to my insulated, chapel-veiled Catholic life. All I knew was that you started your education in those rough Wayne County schools with skanky, hairy arm-pitted girls who fist-fought for their boys—or so we all imagined. Because even in West Virginia—the lowest state in the pecking order—we were desperate for someone to pick on, too. And how quickly those of us who fled this soot, our *backward* heritage, climbed up a rung or two to by donning that nose-thumbing attitude like a new Armani suit—a designer label we assured our metropolitan jetsetters we could *never* find back home, though we could if we had the inclination, I now admit.

Your mother pats your hand and makes cryptic references to your drinking habits. "His life would have turned out so differently if you two were still together." Said as cool and detached as if we'd just broken up six months ago. As if she'd been thinking it every day of her life since then, obliterating your marriage and children, and grandchildren—a fact I still can't fathom as I try to avoid your mother's assessment, the weight of her inference. You certainly drank very little with me, except on our first official date, of course, when you showed up drunk, threw up an hour later, slurred apologies as our double date drove you home and slogged you to the front door to deposit you into your mother's arms—a regular pieta. And the next day, the ungrammatical letter stuck in my locker vent, the plea for forgiveness, the promise to never do it again. And you didn't. In truth, we only traded a legal substance for an illegal one sold in baggies, but at least I didn't have to worry about you driving drunk.

And how you loved to drive. The two of us whipping off somewhere in your GTO, leaving my neglected friends in our dusty wake, the windows down, wind knotting my hair, but I didn't care. A Marlboro dangling from your lip, James Dean, another cause-deprived rebel—a difficult persona to maintain with your mother chasing after you with buckets of chicken livers. Your adrenaline torqued by taunting police, leaving them in a trail of smoke and tread marks—or so you claimed. And the places we went, magical to me, who barely understood our hometown's geography after all those sheltered years on the hill. I certainly knew nothing about the West End, or Kentucky, the state line we crossed at night to park and gawk at oil refineries, the gridwork of lights, flames shooting from columns. Better than fireworks.

I have been in hotels, Tommy. Gaped at spectacular views in New York, Athens, Rome. Still, nothing will compete with a blue muscle car parked before the industrial lightshow that back-dropped our clumsy petting, exploring, your astounding patience. And when it happened, finally, that carnal coupling the trembling nuns taught me to fear, it was neither frightening nor a crescendo of sexual enlightenment. It was sweet, and pure, and probably the most honest moment of that part of my life.

You spoiled me, you know, for other men. Hung me so high in the clouds no one else could reach. Not that anyone tried. In fact, some weren't just content to lasso me back to earth; they wanted to bury me prematurely, too. Which makes your devotion all the more stunning—another secret yearning I will never divulge to my feminist friends.

"Here comes Tommy's oldest," Frances says. She's still gripping my hand.

I pivot my head expecting a skinny boy with a golden halo of hair, cigarette burns on his forearms. He's not a boy any longer, at twenty-four.

Your son is handsome, Tommy. Built like a football player, tall as your father, trim military haircut that is the fashion now. A gold loop in his ear, also trendy. I wonder what you think of him, so *in*, when you were so anti-in. Something I admired about you. Didn't give a shit what anyone thought, were not swayed or cut by popular opinion—an insecurity in myself I still try to rein in. A tendency that makes me prone to reverse snobbery in addition to the usual kind. I think that's what drew us together. Two likeable misfits who meant no harm.

I later learned that our strange pairing raised more than one quizzical eyebrow. Ten years after high school I ran into Kurt Owens at a Milwaukee restaurant. You remember him: our bullshitting classmate voted most likely to be murdered. He was still very much alive and trying to speak in code about how unfathomable it was for a certain brooding, artsy girl to date a certain wiry grease-monkey boy. A conundrum that kept our classmates scratching their heads—though we had no idea anyone gave us a second thought.

Artsy girl must have thought he was a wonderful man, I said to Kurt.

I suppose so, Kurt said, no doubt wondering if that could possibly be the truth. It was. Mostly.

Because we did fight, tried on adult language and scare tactics due mostly to your sullen possessiveness. Like the time you caught your friend, *your* friend, ogling my legs as we tossed Frisbee at the armory. When we got in the car you sped down Spring Valley Drive, that crazy, S-curved mess, driving 90 miles an hour, going airborne as we crested hills. We were flying. But you didn't care, because you were trying to alarm me with the power behind your 440 engine, as if you wanted to smash us into a tree to show the power behind your love. Though I clawed the seats and screamed: "Tommy, slow down!" the truth is, your frightening jealousy thrilled me.

Your son's very pregnant wife plods over lugging a fierce two-year-old who wants his daddy: Now!

"This is Trina," your mother says. "She's expecting in a month."

"How nice," I say, feeling suddenly woozy, overcome by lineage: mother, son, grandson, great-grandson. A generational snapshot that could very well have been mine, at least some genetic version of it. And I remember so well when you called me with your big news. I was a sophomore in college and suddenly bookish, as if someone switched on a siren in my brain that screamed: *Learn!* (Before we broke up, when you called me from Kermit or Pinch, you listened in silence as I blathered on about Ionesco and Beckett, Kant and Kierkegaard. I listened even more silently as you moaned about late shipments of wiper blades and spark plugs. Your incessant pleas: *Move down here. Please!* My stalling answer: *Not yet. Not yet. Not.*)

But the last time we spoke, your wobbly voice in the receiver indicated your drunkenness, the sober hiatus apparently over: *I'm getting married! And she's pregnant!* Like you just won the lottery. I guess you did, because that's everything you ever wanted. More than money, more than car chases, more than fame (a byline in *The Tribune*, for example), you wanted a family. I knew by the way you looked at me that time I held your newborn niece. I saw my squat-kitchened, chain-linked future unfurl in your eyes.

A cluster of new arrivals approach and I try to slide my fingers from Frances's grip.

She holds on tight. "Where are you going." It's not a question, exactly. More like a scolding.

"To the bathroom," I whisper. "I'll be right back."

She doesn't believe me, and with good reason. She relents, though her frown reveals her disappointment in me, in my weakness. I am no stoic grande dame. Thankfully she is engulfed by a circle of fluttering women so I no longer have to suffer her critical eye.

I slink to the wall and skim along it toward an exit, bumping into flower arrangements, statues of cherubs and women balancing burdensome urns on their shoulders. I nearly make it to the door, nearly, when a woman's hand cups my elbow, a penetrating steel clamp.

"Are you Julie?"

I scan her in the same manner she scans me. "Yes."

"I'm Maureen. Tommy's wife."

Oh fuck.

I knew this would happen, eventually, and I look at this woman who looks not *un*like me with her bobbed auburn hair, the practical haircut for middle-aged women.

I take her hand, open my mouth to offer appropriate words, but she offers astonishing ones of her own: "I knew you would be beautiful."

I sputter because, I can tell you this now, late-bloomers never ever feel beautiful. Wait. That's not true. I felt beautiful when you looked into me in a way that no man did before, or has since.

"You're beautiful, too," I say.

"He always liked brunettes," your wife says. A pained laugh before her mouth flattens into a line. "We were divorced, you know."

"I didn't know." That's a lie.

"Four years now."

Maureen waves her hand to encompass every potent thing in this room, including you. "It's a relief in a way. For the kids, especially. Every late night phone call was a scare. And now it's happened. It's over."

I know what she is saying, exactly, though I wonder why she is making this confession to a complete stranger. And then I know, because she delivers one more astonishing fact: "All the time we were married I felt like I was living in your shadow."

It's difficult to breathe and I feel myself tipping backward just a hair, teetering on heels. I have to put one hand out for balance, the other over my mouth to keep from screaming.

"He went to see you, you know."

"What?" I say, conjuring an image of you scrabbling out of O'Hare airport toward the taxi queue, no luggage because there was no time for packing, my address on a scrap of paper clutched in your palm.

"When you came back here to give that speech."

"Oh." I rewind ten years, twelve, and remember that talk at the university which was open to the public. The auditorium crammed with journalism classes forced into attendance, my former professors, old neighbors, my mother, of course. I try to recall faces, look for you standing by the back door, your usual strategy. Did I look right at you and not know it? No. I would have known.

"Did you ever get married?" she asks, eyes boring into mine as if the answer is somehow vital.

"Yes," I say, omitting the fact that this is my fourth go-round, with three exes in three different states.

She lets out a disappointed sigh and peels off the next logical question. "How long?"

My impulse is to give her the combined total, nine years, but I don't. "Richard and I have been together four years." A record for me and he's a perfectly lovely man. Perfectly fine. Who owns a reasonable car and drives at a reasonable speed. But the recently tabulated truth is that we've occupied the same bed for less than 1000 nights. Apparently I am not Scheherazade enough to keep him home. His job requires a certain amount of traveling, wining and dining. A lifestyle I imbibed in and acquiesced to at first because of my own all-consuming career, a vocation I walked away from with one impulsive phone call.

"Any children?"

"Yes. I have a three-year-old daughter."

"Three! You started late."

"I guess I did."

"Well, you had your career already and I'm just starting mine," your wife says. "Once the kids were mostly grown I went to nursing school. Just finished last May."

"Congratulations."

"Sometimes I wish I'd waited to have kids, like you."

I look into her eyes that are spooling backward into the life she shared with you, years filled with diapers and teething, school plays and driving lessons, images that make my stomach clench.

Her eyes pull back into focus, the present, and she says: "What's your daughter's name?"

"Helena."

"I bet she's gorgeous."

I want so much to pull out her photo and show your wife just how beautiful Helena is, a practice I shuddered at as a childless woman. I want her to see my daughter's doleful eyes. It's as if she's trying to steal people's souls when she looks at them, and the first moment I looked at her, I let her steal mine, which is the exact moment I knew I couldn't leave her in the hands of the impeccably referenced nanny Richard and I so painstakingly researched and retained.

"There are advantages to waiting," your wife says. "No money worries, I'm sure. Your husband can probably spend more time at home."

I have to swallow the bubble of laughter caught in my throat, if that's what it is. Helena's soul-stealing magic has not entranced Richard any better than my 1001 tales.

"I bet you have a nice house. Better than the one Tommy and I started out in, I'm sure."

"I do. I mean, I guess I do." A quick vision of the newly developed, upscale, planned community miles from the city. Our custom-built home with the undulating landscaping that secludes us from our neighbors. No chain link, no squat kitchen, but sometimes it presses in just the same. A closeness that occasionally sends my mind reeling backward, too, not all the way to West Virginia, but to the two-bedroom condo I still own in Lincoln Park, with a galley kitchen and a cedar-fenced patch of grass, to the tenant whose lease renews every March, less than six months from now—162 days.

Your wife looks at her shoes, searching for a tactful exit.

"I really need to be going," my gift to her.

"It was good to finally meet you," she says. "It's strange, but it means a lot to me that you came, to know that he still means something to you. That all his pining wasn't for nothing." This extraordinarily generous woman looks over at you, all alone now.

She begins to walk away, but I put my hand on her arm because there is still one thing I need to know. "Was he a good father?"

Your wife looks at me, the tears welling as she weighs everything, and there is a lot to weigh. Finally she tells me what I already suspected. "Yes. He was a wonderful dad."

I nod and watch her walk toward you, maybe to tell you this herself.

I head into the foyer, pass cypress trees and consoling streams, though I don't really see them because of my own blurring tears. I'm not crying for you, Tommy, though I'm sure I will in the months, the years to come. I push out into bright sunlight and start running, of course, the thing that I do. I hop into my SUV, crank the engine and peel out of the parking lot, tires squealing, gravel spraying. I can't buzz down the windows fast enough, all four of them, and when I veer onto the main road I mash my foot against the gas, urging this behemoth to go fast, faster, and though it's no GTO, the speedometer needle shudders as it passes 50-55-60. It's still not fast enough but the wind feels so good, my hair lashing my face, stinging my eyes. I don't care. But I'm not running away, Tommy. I'm running toward something. The same elusive thing that's tumbled me from Dallas to Denver, Seattle to Chicago. The belief that if I just run fast enough I can reach 90 mph and lift off as I crest over hills. Because even after all this time, especially now with you beside me, shit-eating grin slicing your face, wild golden hair whipping, I am still desperate, utterly frantic, to fly.

Get Ready

Chloe and her mother huddled inside Foodland's bus shelter fending off pelting autumn rain. Wet grocery bags smelled like worms, so Chloe burrowed her nose into her mother's side. Sarah's foot tapped fiercely as she willed the bus to arrive: "Come on, come on, come *on*." She balanced a wilting sack against her angular hip until the bottom split and out spilled cans of Spam and tamales, grape soda and 3/$1.00 pork 'n beans. Eggs broke, the jelly jar cracked, and Sarah yowled: "Shit!"

Scrambling to collect the rolling goods, Chloe reached over the curb for the soggy lettuce when a Dodge Ram drove by splashing her with a muddy wave.

Sarah glowered at the truck. "Asshole!" she yelled, pulling Chloe up by the elbow to swipe off loose grass and dead leaves. "Son of a bitch ought to look where he's driving."

They heard heavy footsteps and turned to see a bearded man tromping toward them. Behind him the offending truck sat cockeyed in the parking lot. "I'm sorry!" he said, brows furrowed, eyes taking in the mess that he made. "I didn't see her." He immediately bent to scoop up groceries, tucking cans inside his pockets and zipped jacket.

"Can I give you a ride home?"

Chloe's and her mother's eyes met.

"Please. Your girl's soaking."

Sarah appraised the man's face, his intentions.

"All right," she said. They followed him to the truck where he opened the passenger door. Sarah slid in first, pulling Chloe up beside her.

The man got in and started the truck. "I really am sorry."

Chloe rested her cheek against the foggy window while Sarah shifted toward the driver, her foot madly twitching. At a red light, she looked at him full-faced, tucking a blade of sopping hair behind her ear to expose the swollen cheek. "My name's Sarah."

"Jack," he said, looking over.

Chloe and Sarah were both surprised when he cupped Sarah's face in his hand to inspect the green bruise. "What happened here?"

Sarah pulled away. "Nothing. It's just . . . nothing."

"What. Somebody hit you?"

She crossed her legs. "It's just that he gets so angry sometimes."

Chloe recognized the tone of her mother's lies. The bruise was from a drunken stumble.

"Your husband?"

"No. A friend. We're staying with him until we get back on our feet." She pressed her face into Chloe's kinky red hair.

"He do this a lot? This—friend?"

"Only lately," she said. "He's not used to a child in the house."

Chloe started to protest, but Sarah squeezed her daughter's knee.

Jack gritted his teeth as Sarah gave him directions.

The truck squeaked to a stop and Chloe popped open the door to jump down. Jack pulled food from his pockets to pile in Sarah's cradled arms. "Look," he said, "if things get bad here you give me a call." He pulled a pencil from the dash board and scratched his number on a bean can. "I could put you up for a night or two."

"You better check with your woman before you make offers like that."

"I don't, uh, have—"

"We'll be fine," she said, edging down the seat. "Thanks anyway."

Inside the apartment, Sarah parted the curtains and watched Jack's taillights recede. "Alleluia," she sang. "God *does* provide."

"Are we leaving now?" Chloe asked.

Sarah rubbed her arms to scale off the perpetual chill that encased her. "No, baby. Just a couple more days, though, so get ready."

Get ready meant start looking for treasure so when Sarah said, "Go!" Chloe could scavenge through whatever man's apartment, pocketing silver lighters and pens, gold rings and tie clips, anything shiny she could palm and tuck. At the new place, when they were alone, she'd lift her arms while Sarah dug into pockets and hoods, under shirts and in cuffs, pulling out surprises like Christmas. She'd hug her daughter tight and say, "Good girl, Chloe. That's my good-good girl. Best thing I ever did in my life was have you."

And she meant it so much that the first years of Chloe's life Sarah planted herself in front of her husband's open palm when he went after the baby for crying. When the open palm clenched to a fist, Sarah scooped up the baby and bolted out of the steep mountain hollow that had trapped her in cold shadows her whole life. But he always found them. Court orders couldn't stop him from stalking and threatening. "I don't listen to no piece a paper," he said. "You're still my wife, and that's my kid. However long it takes, Sarah, I'll get her back."

That was enough to scare Sarah from one town to the next, to family, at first, then any marginal friend. After they were used up, she started scrounging up men. Always moving a little farther west, a little closer to sea level to escape the Appalachians, the forest of trees that made her feel as tangled in milkweed and kudzu as they were. If she could just get to flat land where the horizon was a straight line that stretched for miles and miles and miles maybe she would feel safe. Maybe the blazing sun would dry up the chronic dampness in her bones. But even when she crossed the Ohio River and made it to Cincinnati, then beyond it to Indianapolis, she still looked over her shoulder. "However long it takes," scraped through her mind.

By now Sarah was used to trading herself for shelter. Her body became a cash crop—her only commodity. It was a business with only a pretense of emotions involved. And as for Chloe, the men pretended to care about her as long as Sarah pretended to care about them. A few months were about as long as the pretense would hold, but before she left one man, she had to line up another. Which had been particularly difficult this time—until Jack. Three days after the grocery store, Sarah's voice crackled into his phone, "He kicked us out." Jack picked them up on a corner six blocks away, their suitcase and clothes bulging and clanking with hidden spoils he did not hear over his continued rail against any man who would strike a woman.

Twenty minutes later they parked in front of Jack's frame house. Sarah pressed Chloe's hand as they stepped onto his porch. Inside, Sarah nodded toward the silver spoon collection on one living room wall, a framed twenty-dollar bill on another. Chloe gawked at an albino deer head mounted over the couch. Its pink eyes scared her and she wanted to run. She swiveled to look at the other walls covered with stuffed fish and birds, thumb-tacked pictures of gorillas, hyenas, zebras.

Chloe gaped at animal pictures lining the hall as Jack led them to a door in the middle. "Here you go," he said, pushing it open, flipping on the light.

Ballerina posters crowded lemon walls. Lace curtains draped the windows. Canopy bed pushed to one side. Chloe backed into her mother's legs.

"What a sweet room," Sarah said, nudging Chloe inside.

Chloe resisted, saying in a wobbly voice, "Whose room is this?"

"My daughter's."

"Your daughter's?" Sarah said, pulling Chloe back against her.

Chloe pressed a plump cheek into her mother's side. "Won't she get mad if I sleep in here?"

Jack leaned in to scan the room. "Camille's away at college. Besides, she hasn't lived here for a long, long time."

Sarah winked, so Chloe went into this other girl's room while Jack led Sarah farther down the hall.

Sarah was surprised by Jack's room. Needlepoint. Dried flowers. Chenille bedspread.

Jack read her expression. "My ex-wife did the decorating. I've just never gotten around to changing it."

Sarah said, "Oh." What startled her even more was when Jack said, "I'll take the couch," and pulled the door closed behind him. Usually the men started in right away, but Sarah was grateful for a night alone, a chance to rifle through Jack's dresser, to heft the mason jar full of half dollars and state quarters to her chest and judge the weight. She grabbed a fistful and slipped them in her pocket before sliding the jar back. A silver picture frame rested on the nightstand. Inside the frame, a much younger Jack sat on porch steps hugging a young girl tightly between his knees, his chin on her head. They both grinned at the camera. The photographer's shadow climbed up the steps beside them.

Sarah needn't have worried. By the second night Jack was back in his bed. With his arms buckled around her, Sarah fell asleep facing west knowing she and Chloe were safe, at least for the time being.

While Jack worked in town, Sarah rummaged through every cabinet, every cupboard, cataloguing treasure for later. Chloe watched TV and listened for the man—Jack—so she could stay out of his way.

"Don't get too close to these guys," her mother always warned. "You never know what they're thinking."

Sarah left Chloe alone so she could find handy pawn shops and bars. She wore pink eye shadow and lipstick for anemic effect, baggy pants that rode her hip bones to accentuate her frailty. She knew the kind of vulnerability that made a man want to protect a woman. *This is for Chloe,* she chanted to herself. But once she had a palm full of dollars, she grew anxious to edge into the thin darkness of bars, the close dampness that assuaged an inner tug she refused to name. After years of running and wheedling, Sarah craved that fuzzy edge of sober. She felt an ironic sense of stability with those barstool silhouettes she would only know for an hour, a day, a week—long enough to make connections, but not long enough for the kudzu to entangle her feet.

At the house, Chloe rested her arms and head on the front windowsill wondering when her mother would return. Jack's narrow road was vaulted with trees, leaves red-yellow-orange-green. Occasionally a car drove by, or a neighbor slapped out a screen door to get mail. Suddenly the sound of laughter and feet smacking concrete spilled onto the street. Chloe pressed her ear to the glass as it grew louder and louder. A herd of school children galloped around the corner chasing, tugging, swinging lunch boxes and book bags. Chloe forgot her mother's standing order to never go outside alone and ran out as they passed. They pulled her along like a parade, but quickly turned the corner, leaving only the echo of footsteps.

From behind her Jack said, "Chloe?"

She twisted around, surprised to see him home this early. "Did you see that?"

"The kids?"

She nodded.

"Power's out in over half the city. We all got to go home. Looks like they hate school as much as I did."

It didn't look like they hated school to Chloe.

"How come you're not in school?"

Chloe shrugged.

Jack's mouth scrunched up on one side. "We still got electric?"

Chloe nodded.

"Where's your mom?"

Chloe looked at her feet. "Gone."

He paused. "I'll be out back," he said, then he jammed his hands in his pockets and left.

Chloe watched clock hands spin round and round. She couldn't read numbers, but the sun was gone, and her mother wasn't back. She smeared peanut butter and jelly on white bread, mashed the pieces together, and was headed to the TV when a curious humming drew her out back. She tracked the noise to the garage, to Jack, covered in wood shavings and dust, sitting in front of a monstrous machine. When he looked up at Chloe the noise stopped.

"What are you doing out here?" he asked.

"Nothing."

He pointed to the lathe. "See this?"

She nodded.

"Never touch. It'll bite your hand clean off." The noise started so abruptly Chloe dropped her sandwich in the dirt, ran back to the house and into her mother, just returning. Sarah handed Chloe a baggie filled with gumballs before wobbling to the garage.

Chloe carried her prize to the good spot she'd found for watching TV.

During *Cop Stories* Jack and Sarah clomped into the kitchen. Fresh coffee smells perked through the house.

"Where I go is my business," Sarah said.

"I didn't say where. I said who."

"Nobody you have to worry about."

"Do I look worried? I'm just asking. Besides, Chloe was alone here, and anyway how come she's not in school?"

"Chloe's been tested gifted," Sarah said without pause. "She's on a waiting list for a special school."

Jack started to speak when the phone rang.

Sarah leaned against the wall and crossed her arms.

Jack said, "Hello?" He listened for a moment then stretched the phone cord out to the back stoop. Sarah strained to hear, always afraid it might be her ex no matter how many states or rivers separated them, but all she heard was low laughter and Jack's last line, "Sorry. It's just not a good time."

Sarah cracked her knuckles. "Who was that?"

"I guess if you can have secrets, so can I." Jack walked past her into the living room where Chloe stared at the TV. "You sure watch a lot of this stuff."

Chloe furrowed her eyebrows. "Yeah?"

He plopped beside her and watched two men in leather punching, stabbing, kicking a man in a suit. They crammed him into a car trunk, slammed the lid down, and shot round after round through the metal and into the man inside, all the while laughing like lunatics. Chloe's round eyes readily took in the violence. Jack grabbed the remote and flipped channels, stopping at a jackrabbit darting oblivious through the desert until a hawk swooped down, nabbed it by the scruff, and carried it up into blue sky.

"Might as well learn something useful," Jack said, but Chloe's round eyes looked the same as when the two leather men shot up the third in the trunk.

Afterwards, whenever Jack found Chloe at the TV, he'd switch stations looking for animals. If there weren't any, he'd shut the thing off and hand her a stack of *National Geographic*. "Look at these," he'd say. "Or go do something. Play." Now Chloe hunted nature shows all by herself, and started her own eye-level gallery of animal pictures down the hall. She clipped photos of snakes wedged under rocks that could easily tip. Birds nested on precarious cliffs, or high up in trees that the wind might blow down.

Three weeks into their stay, Sarah pulled a tattered tablecloth from the back of the china cabinet and draped it over a chair back. "Look at this, Chloe," she said, eyes roving over the ancient piece of handiwork. "Beautiful," Sarah whispered, running her fingertips lightly over the embroidery and openwork stitch. "Moths got to it in a few places," she said, sliding her hand underneath to expose the open wounds.

"Bet you could fix it," Chloe said.

"You think?"

Chloe nodded and soon Sarah was sitting on the couch with the tablecloth fanned out before her like a wedding dress. Chloe sat beside her mother holding the thread and scissors, begging to sew just one stitch. "Okay," Sarah said. "But let me show you how first." Chloe watched her mother's thin fingers, how she deftly wove the needle between the fragile fabric. "Aunt Nellie taught me how to sew."

Chloe scrunched up her face. "I don't remember her."

"Sure you do. Don't you remember the time—" Sarah stopped sewing and looked at her daughter. "I guess you don't," Sarah said.

"And it's a shame. She's about the only thing I really miss from back home." Sarah's gaze drifted over into a corner and stayed there for so long that Chloe looked over expecting to find a mouse or a cricket.

"Mama?" she said, to break the spell.

Sarah shook off whatever memory captivated her. "Now you try," Sarah said, standing to drape the cloth over Chloe's knees. Chloe bit her lip in concentration as she worked the needle this way and that. "That's good!" Sarah said. Chloe looked up, smiling, and over her mother's shoulder saw Jack looking on in silence. He held a finger to his lips for secrecy. "You're doing fine," Sarah continued. "You know you're brilliant, don't you," she said. "Course you get that from me." Chloe giggled, peering at Jack, who quietly watched the mother-daughter tableau, his head tilted to the side, eyes droopy and warm. It was a look Chloe had never seen on a man's face.

That night, while Sarah and Jack laughed in their room, Chloe snuck out to the garage. She hadn't forgotten the forbidden machine. She tiptoed around it, mesmerized by moonlit edges and angles. Curious about this hand-eating contraption, she eased a pointed finger down to tease when the overhead lights flipped on. Jerking her hand straight up in the air, she would have run except Jack leaned in the doorway with a hand on his hip and an amused smile slicing through his beard. Chloe backed against his tool chest, fully prepared for a slap or punch. Jack seemed to be deciding something, and finally said, "Hard to resist, isn't it. Come on, I'll show you how she goes."

And he did. More than nature shows, it became her favorite pastime as Chloe watched the miracle of turning two-by-twos into chair arms and legs, or spindles for rockers or banisters. Half-finished projects crowded the garage walls and hung from the ceiling. Jack sat with his head cocked to the side. He'd position a length of chalked cherry or mahogany between the two clamps. Round and round it spun with a hum while Jack shaped and sanded. Leaning his tools into its surface, he could change the machine's whine while molding splintery, hard-edged wood into something so smooth Chloe often sat for hours turning it over and over in her soft palms. They rarely spoke while at the lathe, but both tried to match the lathe's song: Jack's hum low and steady, Chloe's high with interrupted breaths.

One Sunday evening Sarah peeked in the garage just as Chloe scooted her stool closer to Jack's. It was a closeness that made Sarah uneasy, made her legs feel itchy, as if something was trying to crawl up and grab hold. When she went back into the house the phone screamed and she barked into it: "Hello!"

"Is Jack there?" It was a woman.

Sarah paused. "Hold on," she said, and stomped back outside, tamping down the earth so that nothing could push through and reach out.

Sarah and Chloe followed Jack to the kitchen where he picked up the receiver. "Yeah?"

He listened. "Can it wait? I'm in the middle of something." A pause. "All right. I'll be over in a minute." He scratched his ear and looked at Chloe. "Sorry kid, gotta go." He looked at Sarah. "My ex-wife's got a busted faucet. I'll be back in an hour or so, okay?"

Sarah leaned against the kitchen wall. "Sure."

Jack tugged on his coat and hefted a toolbox from the closet. He kissed Sarah's forehead before leaving. From the window, she watched him climb into the truck. Tilting the rear view mirror, he raked fingers through his hair and beard. By the time he backed out of the driveway, Sarah had slid on pink eye shadow, lipstick, and her oversized coat.

Jack did return in an hour. Sarah did not.

Harsh voices filled Chloe's dreams before yanking her fully awake.

Sarah and Jack argued outside her door.

"She was here all alone, for God's sake. Anything could have happened."

Sarah strained most of the slur from her voice. "Nothing *did* happen." A hint of guilt edged the words. "And it's *still* none of your damn business where I go."

"Did I ask? All I said was I don't like Chloe left alone in my house." Sarah spouted the line that usually bought more time. "You want us to leave? Fine. We'll be out tomorrow if that's really what you want."

"That's *not* what I want, Sarah. But if you can't stay and look after your child, maybe you *should* go."

"Fine. We'll leave in the morning." Her footsteps padded down the hall.

Jack kicked the floor board beside Chloe's door. "Shit," he said, and walked the other way.

Sarah hugged her knees tight in Jack's bed. She'd been kicked out before, but never for this. Never for leaving Chloe by herself. It was a puzzle she couldn't quite solve, so her mind turned to her immediate problem: she had no real money and no place yet to go.

In the morning Chloe found Jack asleep on the couch. She leaned close to his face, crinkled from sleep and from time. The thick hand on his chest was road-mapped with veins, but she knew the palm would be shiny smooth with calluses from molding all that wood. She looked at her rubbery pink palms wondering when her own calluses would form.

Chloe slipped back into her room and scanned the bright walls, Camille's walls, *her* canopy bed, *her* desk, *her* ballerina posters. She imagined Jack tucking his daughter in night after night after night. Laughing and whispering until she fell asleep. In the morning when

Camille awoke it would all still be hers.

Chloe crept into Jack's room and dug under the covers beside her mother.

Sarah rolled toward her. "Morning, baby," she said. "Sleep well?"

"Yep."

"Least somebody did."

Sarah pulled herself up against the headboard. "Where's Jack?"

"On the couch."

"Well Chloe," she said, sliding fingers through her hair, "we've been here awhile already, so I guess it's time to—"

"Mama, I got something to show you." She dangled a baggie filled with wadded bills and loose change. "It was in the middle of the sidewalk, so I just ran out and took it. Finders keepers, right? Nobody saw me, so finders keepers, right?"

Sarah snatched the baggie. "Absolutely."

Chloe hadn't found the cash. It was an accumulation of birthday and Christmas money from various men. A quarter or fifty cents pressed into her palm to get her out of the house for half an hour alone with her mother. Chloe instinctively hoarded the handouts, couch nickels, sidewalk pennies, for some future purpose which had never become clear—until now.

Sarah dumped the money between them and counted crinkled fives and ones. "Wonder how much there is."

Giddy, Chloe blurted, "Can we stay?"

Sarah stopped counting.

"I mean, just a little while longer?"

Sarah took a deep breath. "Look, Chloe, what do I keep telling you about getting too close to these guys."

"I know," Chloe mumbled.

Sarah scooped the money back in the bag and sat perfectly still. "Brrrr!" she finally said, sliding out of bed to squint out the window.

"Looks like winter's coming early."

Chloe followed and looked outside at the frosty glaze coating the grass and tulip poplar out back. Steam rising from the garage roof.

Sarah smoothed her daughter's sleep-tangled hair. "I wouldn't mind staying put until spring."

Chloe looked up at her mother. "You mean it?"

"It's not up to me, you know. There's Jack."

"He'll say yes, Mama, I know it."

"We'll see. But this isn't forever, okay? This isn't forever."

"I know."

"Now go to your room for awhile. Jack and I need to have a little talk."

Chloe skipped to her room, but paused to watch her mother pad to the living room, kneel beside Jack, and slide her hand up his T-shirt. He rolled toward her and Sarah buried her face in his beard.

"I'm sorry," she said. "I'll stay home with Chloe."

For the most part she did.

Sarah sat from morning till noon, eyes ping-ponging from Chloe to the front door, foot twitching against the viny green fingers threatening to tug at Sarah's feet. She tried to sound excited when Chloe found another picture of a rabbit hutch, lion's den, eagle's nest. "That's real nice, honey. No, I'm sure it's safe or they wouldn't build them up that high."

Afternoons were rough when the luring sun glared bright outside, and the thick pull of the bars was unyielding. Sarah paced the house, shredding frenzied trails of tissues until she relented and yanked on her coat. "I'll just be a sec, okay? I'm going to the corner, so don't answer the phone, all right?" She'd plant a hard kiss on her daughter's head and yell, "Be right back!" before closing the door.

Heavy snow fell the first Saturday of December. "Guess this is the day," Jack said. "Everybody grab your coats."

Chloe lay belly down on the living room floor, coloring. "What for?"

"Christmas tree hunting."

"Isn't it kind of early?" Sarah asked. She huddled under a thick blanket on the couch, feet pummeling the cushions.

"Gotta get our tree before all the good ones are gone."

"You go. We'll stay here where it's warm," Sarah said, swaddling the blanket around her.

Jack tilted his head. "Aw, come on. I haven't done this in years."

"I'll go!" Chloe said, standing.

"I don't think so," Sarah said. "It's pretty nasty outside."

"Let her come," Jack said.

"Please, Mama?"

"Didn't you hear me? I said no."

Jack looked at Sarah, then tugged Chloe's earlobe. "Sorry, kid. I'll pick us out a good one." He zipped his coat and went outside.

Chloe bit her lower lip, scowling, as she listened to Jack scraping the truck windows outside.

"Don't give me that look," Sarah said. "Tell you what. We'll have our own fun. Want me to paint your fingernails?" She stood, draped the blanket over her shoulders, and headed down the hall. "Now where'd I put that stuff? It's got glitter in it!" she yelled from the bathroom.

Chloe didn't wait for her mother to find it; she snatched her coat and ran outside.

Jack was sliding the truck in gear when Chloe opened the passenger door.

"She changed her mind?" he said.

Chloe looked straight ahead. "Uh huh."

They wove through slushy streets to lot after lot. "Too scrawny.

Too bare. It leans," Jack kept saying. But after they loaded the perfect blue spruce in his truck, Jack blew on his fingers and said, "You want hot chocolate?"

"Sure!" Chloe said, head bobbing.

Inside Benny's Donuts, Jack thawed his fingers over the steamy cocoa. Laverne, the waitress, slid a Santa cookie in front of Chloe. "On the house," Laverne said.

"Really?" Chloe said.

"If it's okay with your dad."

Chloe expected Jack to correct the mistake. All he said was, "Okay by me."

Chloe swiveled on her bar stool, dunking marshmallows, trying to decipher this new warm bubble in her stomach, her chest.

Jack sensed her joy. "I'm glad your mom let you come."

Chloe stopped swiveling. The bubble popped, spilling a bitter liquid inside her. She opened and closed her mouth twice before whispering, "She didn't."

"What?"

"I never picked out a tree before."

Jack clinked his spoon against the mug. "Your mom is really going to be pissed."

Chloe whispered, "I know."

"At me, too."

She looked up at him. "You?" The liquid in her belly turned into acid that burned.

Laverne leaned over the counter. "Anything else?"

"No." Jack slid a five from his wallet. "Well wait, Chloe. Why don't we get your mom a peace offering? Maybe a cake with lots of flowers and swirls?"

"We got a real pretty poinsettia cake over here. You like that?" Laverne asked.

Chloe nodded.

Laverne pulled out the cake and set it before them. "You want any writing on it?"

"What do you think, Chloe?"

"How about, World's Best Mama, Love Chloe and Jack."

Jack laughed. "That ought to soften her up."

"Can you do it in pink?" Chloe asked. "Mama likes pink."

"Sure, honey," Laverne said. "And I'll do it right here so you can watch." She grabbed a frosting tube and squeezed out bright pink gel, calling out each letter as she wrote. "Now you're gonna have to help me with the Chloe part. How do you spell that name?" She looked at Jack, who looked at Chloe.

"How do you spell your name?" he asked.

Chloe pressed her hands out flat on the counter.

"It's okay, sugar," Laverne said. "You wanna write it yourself?" She held out the tube.

Chloe reached out, but pushed it away. "I don't want to."

Jack looked at Chloe, but said to Laverne, "Just take your best shot."

Sarah rubbed her red hands as she paced before the picture window. She'd gone outside without gloves or coat, circling the neighborhood in search of Chloe. "God," she said. When Jack's truck pulled in the driveway, she leaned against the window straining to see inside the cab. There she was. "Thank God," Sarah said. Jack got out and opened Chloe's door. Reaching in he drew out a white box. Chloe hopped down and walked behind him, feet dragging through the snow.

When the front door opened, Jack said, "You should have come, Sarah, we had a great time."

Sarah pushed past him, knelt down, and hugged her daughter. "I was afraid your father—" She squeezed Chloe, then held her at arm's length. "Don't you *ever* go off without me. You hear?"

Chloe mumbled, "Yeah."

"You hear me!"

"Yes!"

Sarah stood. "And you," she said to Jack. "Don't ever take my daughter anywhere without me."

"We wanted you to come, Sarah. And you know I'd never let anything happen to her. She's like my own kid."

Sarah's cold eyes drilled into his. "She's *not* yours."

"All right, all right," he said, thrusting the cake forward. "Here. We brought you a present."

Instead of grabbing the box, Sarah grabbed Chloe's hand and yanked her down the hall.

Jack held the cake and watched Sarah recede. "You're welcome."

Chloe ripped into her third pack of tinsel. Jack slipped a wire hook onto a gold ornament and handed it to Sarah.

"You ever hear from Chloe's special school?" Jack asked.

Chloe hesitated, but threw another wad of tinsel high up on the tree and watched it slide down.

Sarah buried the gold ball deep inside the tree. "They said we probably wouldn't hear until summer."

"I see." He paused. "Cause Wilson Elementary is just a few blocks over and I hear it's pretty good. Some of the guys at work have kids there. They say it's all right."

"Waste of time," Sarah said.

"I don't know. I mean, she's gonna be eight—"

"I know how old Chloe's gonna be. Don't you think I know how old my own daughter is?"

He handed her a red star. "Yes. It's just that I thought maybe she could start in January when the other kids go back. Might give her a head sta—"

"I do the thinking for Chloe. I'm still her mother, so quit trying to buddy up to—"

Chloe stopped flinging tinsel when Jack rose and grabbed both of her mother's wrists. Sarah tried to pull free, but Jack held tight.

"Let go!" Sarah yelled.

Jack leaned close to her face. "I *do* have an ulterior motive. If Chloe's in school down the street, you'll both have to stick around me for a good long time." He held her arms behind her, kissing her hard and fast on the mouth. "Got it?" He let go and settled back down to hook ornaments. Sarah stood with her arms still behind her. Jack handed over a reindeer made of pipe cleaners and spools. "Now get busy, woman. We got a heap a tree to cover."

Chloe smiled wide and threw tinsel even higher up the tree.

Sarah slid into hot bath water with a wince. Inhaling deeply, she marveled that the tree's pine scent lingered even here. The faucet eked a slow drip-drip. Sounds of sawing and hammering drifted through the window, sounds that had persisted all day. Earlier, Sarah went out back, snooping, but Chloe hollered: "Stay out!"

"Elf work," Jack added. "Sorry, ma'am."

Sitting back in the tub, Sarah felt warmth penetrate down to marrow. It surprised her. She had grown used to the deep chill that no sweater, blanket, or thermostat would ease. But today the chill was gone.

Sliding under water, quiet pressure clamped against her ears. Only here could she allow the thought to mature, Jack's thought planted with four nothing words. "A good long time." Sarah pushed a bubble from her mouth. It rose to the surface and burst with a possibility of permanence she hadn't considered for years.

In the bedroom, Sarah lifted Jack's photo from the nightstand and ran her fingers along its cool frame. She studied the two images. Jack and his daughter fit tight like a puzzle. How easy it looked, this close-ness, this bond, and how safe. She traced the photographer's shad-ow that crept up beside them. Maybe it's me, she thought, trying to squeeze inside.

On a Friday after dinner Sarah ran her fingertip along Jack's jaw. "I have to talk to you," she said, "in the bedroom." She wanted to cel-ebrate her first sober day.

Chloe set down her milk glass. "But Jack, we have to finish the—you know!"

Jack kissed Sarah's palm. "We can work on that later, Chloe."

Sarah wrapped her hand around Jack's wrist and teased him to-ward the bedroom, toward the silver-framed photo.

Chloe painted her third miniature shutter when Jack creaked into the garage.

"How's it going?" he said.

She stopped painting. "So-so."

He eyed the birdhouse, Chloe's gift idea, an exact replica of his own house right down to yellow siding, green shutters, red roof.

"Looks great to me," he said, ignoring the paint runs and missed patches.

"You sure it won't blow down?" she asked.

Jack rolled the metal pole on the ground with his foot. He planned to cement it into the ground come spring. "That baby's not going anywhere."

Chloe grinned and dabbed her brush into paint.

Four days before Christmas Sarah lay on the couch; the dim glow of the lit tree soothed her. In the kitchen, Jack and Chloe washed the supper dishes. Their low murmurs and laughter floated around

Sarah, lulling her toward sleep.

"Sarah," Jack said, easing her back a notch.

She opened one eye.

"Listen," he said. "I have to go over to my ex-wife's for a little while."

This pulled her back several more notches. "What for?"

"She called me at work today." He paused for an interruption, but there was none. "Seems Camille's not coming home for Christmas like she'd planned." He draped the dish towel over his shoulder. "My ex is pretty upset, so I said I'd drop by."

All Sarah could push out was, "Oh."

"I won't be long." He bent down to kiss her. "Go on back to sleep."

Sarah rolled over but did not fall asleep. Instead she tried to untangle the new knot balled up in her chest.

Several hours later Jack's key scratched in the front lock. Sarah lay in bed listening as he tiptoed in the darkness, emptied his pockets on the dresser, slipped off his clothes. Under covers, he lay on his side, body curving away from her.

Sarah waited for his rhythmic breath, then rolled toward his bare shoulder. She reached over to raise the cover, sweeping her fingers through the back of his hair. It was damp. Leaning close, she smelled the fragrance of newly washed hair, his body soaped suspiciously clean.

She rolled away, fists clenched, mind crowded with images of Jack and his ex-wife together. The chill that had so recently vanished gripped her and bore through to marrow. "God," she whispered, certain her breath misted white in the frigid air.

In the morning Sarah feigned sleep when Jack slipped from the bed, the house, and his truck echoed down the street. She tried to push off the covers, but the blankets tangled around her feet like dense underbrush. Finally she freed herself, swung her legs over the bed, and reached to turn on the ceramic lamp. Instead she swatted it to the floor where it split in two, one half laying in a white patch of sunlight filtering in from the west.

Chloe scuffed into the kitchen as her mother yelled into the phone. "Just for a few days. Okay. Okay! Never mind."

Chloe pulled a chair to the counter to reach the Captain Crunch. She carried the box to the TV, turned it on, but did not watch. All morning she listened to her mother dial and redial, plead and curse. It was all too familiar but Chloe hoped she was wrong. When Sarah stepped beside her, eyelids and lips coated pink, she knew.

"I'll be back in a little while," she said. "So get—" She didn't finish. Just shivered, turned the thermostat to high, and left.

Air in the house was so thick Chloe could barely pull it into her lungs. She trudged from room to room for a fresh breath, but found none. Finally she raced to the garage where the air was thin and crisp and carried smells of wood shavings and earth. Sitting on Jack's stool she spun around and around until she had to hold onto the lathe to keep from falling. She stood dizzily and fell into piles of sawdust and wood fragments. On the cool ground, she closed her eyes and groped blindly for a smooth wood scrap. She found one and held it to her nose, inhaled the raw scent, and rubbed it against her cheek.

"Are you all right?" Jack said, kneeling beside her.

She opened her eyes. "Yeah."

He looked her over, brushing bits of wood from her hair. "What are you doing on the floor?"

"I was hot," she said, as he helped her up.

He scanned the garage, puzzled. "Where's your mother?"

Chloe looked at the wood scrap in her hand. "I think she went to the store."

"How come she didn't take you?"

"I didn't want to go." She hated lying.

Jack scratched his jaw. "Look, Chloe. I've got some work to do out here, so why don't you go back inside."

"Can I help?"

"Nope. Elf work. Strictly confidential." He started sifting through the wood pile for a particular piece. "Go on, now."

She plodded toward the door and paused. "Jack?"

"Yeah?" he said without looking.

She wanted so badly to tell him something, anything, but couldn't link the thoughts to words. "Nothing." She slipped the wood scrap in her pocket and left.

Chloe sat on the couch facing the tree that dripped silver, gold, orange, red, blue. Packages spilled from beneath it labeled *Sarah* and *Chloe*. To the side was the birdhouse wound with aluminum foil, a red bow taped to the top. Chloe listened to Jack's sawing and banging. Inside her something was being built too. She didn't know what but it grew with each pound of the hammer, each pull of the saw.

The sun slid from the sky, straining every hint of color from the room. Chloe slipped down to plug in the tree. She lay on the floor looking at light slivers reflected on the ceiling. Suddenly the lathe sliced through the darkness outside and in. Chloe caught and echoed its rhythm with her high, unsteady hum. She wondered if Jack was humming, too. A truck rattled down their street, shaking windows, vibrating the tree. Light fragments shivered on the ceiling, then steadied. Chloe scooted toward the tree and slid her foot between packages to feel its rough trunk. Pressing her foot against bark, she gave a slight nudge that shivered the fragments again. Tapping lightly she matched the shiver to her song and the lathe's. Faster or slower, she tapped to keep pace, until she wasn't keeping pace any longer. Her own song grew louder and louder as she banged the tree harder.

The ceiling rippled with light waves of color. The tree wobbled back and forth, ornaments clinking, some dropping. Each time it rocked toward her, Chloe held out her arms, not to protect, but to embrace the spiky branches should they fall.

"What the hell are you doing!" The overhead light flipped on.

"What the *hell* are you doing!" Her mother wrenched her upright by the arm. "Where's Jack?"

"Out back."

"Good." Sarah wiped at makeup smudged around her eyes. "Look, I've got a place lined up, so get ready."

Chloe didn't move.

"Go on," Sarah said. "We have to hurry."

Chloe looked around the room. "But I thought we were going to—"

"What! Stay here?" She let out a laugh. "Jack's just another guy. That's all he ever was," she said, though she couldn't look at her daughter.

Chloe paused, then nudged a present with her toe. "What about Christmas?"

"Don't *worry* about Christmas," Sarah said. "We'll take the whole damn thing with us!" She went to the front closet and yanked Chloe's jacket from a hanger. "Here. Go get Jack's room. I'll take care of all this."

Numbly, mechanically, Chloe trudged down the hall. In Jack's room, her eyes roamed from one shiny object to the next. There was his pocket knife, wrist watch, tie pin centered with a real diamond. She slid them into her coat pocket and heaved the coin jar to her stomach with both hands.

In the living room, her mother ripped open presents, shoving their contents into a green lawn bag. She held up the Amateur Wood Carving Kit. "Cool, huh? It's for you." She crammed it inside. Lying sideways was the birdhouse only partially unwrapped. Sarah saw Chloe eye the gift. "I'm sorry," she said. "It's just too heavy to take." Chloe still stared at the sturdy house. "It's real nice, though. Thanks, honey. Now hurry and get the stuff in the kitchen."

Chloe did not move.

Sarah said, "Go on."

"But what about—"

"Santa? Oh, don't worry. I got Santa's shit, too," and grinning, she patted the bag.

"No! It's—"

"What! What the hell more do you want? We got Christmas!"

Chloe stood rigid for several seconds, then threw down the coin jar, scattering Kennedy half dollars and glinting state quarters and glass shards across the floor. She held her mother's startled stare then bolted to the kitchen.

"Don't you dare!" Sarah said, giving chase.

Chloe scrambled for the back door yelling, "I don't want to go! I don't want to go!"

The lathe abruptly stopped and Jack bellowed from the garage, "Chloe?"

Sarah lunged and caught her daughter around the waist.

"No!" Chloe screamed, stretching, fingertips just grazing the doorknob before Sarah jerked her back.

Yanking her daughter through the house, Sarah scooped up her suitcase and lugged it and Chloe out the front door, down the steps, onto icy concrete. Holding tight, she dragged them too fast down the street. Chloe stumbled and scrambled to steady herself, but her mother would not stop until they were three blocks away. Spinning to face her, for the first time in her life Sarah slapped Chloe across the face, splitting her lip. Chloe staggered backward and fell against gnarled roots.

"Never again, do you hear me? Don't you *ever* run from me again."
Chloe stood, cupping her mouth, gritting her teeth to keep from crying. Sarah again grabbed the suitcase and Chloe's wrist, pulling them several streets farther to a black Lincoln parked in a boarded up Chevron station.

Sarah opened the back door, pushing Chloe and the suitcase inside. The man behind the wheel twisted around. Beneath the dome light he saw blood spilling from Chloe's lip, red welts outlining her jaw.

"What happened to her?"

Sarah got in and slammed the door. "Jack. Couldn't catch me, so he beat on my child."

The man turned back around to start the car. "Bastard," he snarled. "Ought to kick his ass."

They drove down Jack's street toward the new man's place. Jack's Christmas tree flickered in the front window; bright blobs of tinsel shimmered in colored light. Beside it stood Jack, mouth open, hands on his hips, looking down at the wreckage on the floor. Chloe craned to watch him angle smaller and smaller until they turned the corner and he was gone.

She sat rigid in the back seat, looking straight at her mother who already nuzzled the new man's neck. Chloe pressed her back into cold vinyl. The blood on her tongue tasted metallic. A hammer. A chisel. Jack's lathe. She licked her lip and closed her eyes tight. Shoving hands into pockets she felt Jack's stolen treasures. She reached over, rolled down the window just a crack, and slipped them outside one by one. The only thing she kept was the smooth wood scrap she'd found in the garage. Slowly she turned it over and over in her palm, forming calluses. She didn't know she was humming until her mother reached back and pinched her knee. But she did not stop.

MARIE MANILLA, a West Virginia native, is a graduate of the Iowa Writers' Workshop. Her stories have appeared in *The Chicago Tribune, Prairie Schooner, Mississippi Review, Calyx Journal, Kestrel, Portland Review, GSU Review,* and other journals. She is the author of the upcoming novel *Shrapnel,* a winner of the Fred Bonnie Award for Best First Novel.